Com. to the Peace conference at Washington

Report of the Kentucky Commissioners

to the late Peace conference held at Washington City

Com. to the Peace conference at Washington

Report of the Kentucky Commissioners
to the late Peace conference held at Washington City

ISBN/EAN: 9783337220747

Printed in Europe, USA, Canada, Australia, Japan

Cover: Foto ©Andreas Hilbeck / pixelio.de

More available books at **www.hansebooks.com**

KENTUCKY COMMISSIONERS

TO THE LATE

PEACE CONFERENCE HELD AT WASHINGTON CITY,

MADE TO THE LEGISLATURE OF KENTUCKY.

FRANKFORT, KY.:
PRINTED AT THE YEOMAN OFFICE
JNO. B. MAJOR, STATE PRINTER.
1861.

MAJORITY REPORT.

WASHINGTON, February 28, 1861.

To His Excellency, Beriah Magoffin, Governor of Kentucky:

The undersigned, Commissioners appointed by a resolution of the General Assembly of the Commonwealth of Kentucky, to meet such Commissioners as might be appointed by the several States in accordance with the request of the State of Virginia, to confer together upon the present condition of our country, respectfully report.

That they assembled in the city of Washington on the 4th inst., twenty-one States being represented, and continued in session until the 27th inst., and finally agreed on the inclosed printed propositions as a basis of settlement and pacification. The journal of our proceedings, as soon as completed and printed, will be transmitted as part of this report.

Respectfully,

> JAMES GUTHRIE,
> C. S. MOREHEAD,
> JOSHUA F. BELL,
> C. A. WICKLIFFE.

P. S.—It is proper to remark, that before this report was written and signed, two of the Commissioners, Hon. J. B. Clay and Gen. Butler, had left the city.

REPORT OF COMMITTEE.—ARTICLE 13.

SECTION 1. In all the present territory of the United States, not embraced within the limits of the Cherokee treaty grant, north of a line from east to west on the parallel of 36 degrees 30 minutes north latitude, involuntary servitude, except in punishment of crime, is prohibited whilst it shall be under a Territorial government; and in all the present territory south of said line, the status of persons owing service or labor as it now exists shall not be changed by law while such territory shall be under a Territorial government; and neither Congress nor the Territorial government shall have power to hinder or prevent the taking to said territory of persons held to labor or involuntary service, within the United States, according to the laws or usages of the State from which such persons may be taken, nor to impair the rights arising out of said relations, which shall be subject to judicial cognizance in the federal courts, according to the common law; and when any territory north or south of said line, within such boundary as Congress may prescribe, shall contain a population required for a member of Congress, according to the then federal ratio of representation, it shall, if its form of government be republican, be admitted into the Union on an equal footing with the original States, with or without involuntary service or labor, as the constitution of such new State may provide.

SECTION 2. Territory shall not be acquired by the United States, unless by treaty; nor, except for naval and commercial stations and depots, unless such treaty shall be ratified by four fifths of all the members of the Senate.

SECTION 3. Neither the Constitution, nor any amendment thereof, shall be construed to give Congress power to regulate, abolish, or control, within any State or Territory of the United States, the relation established or recognized by the laws thereof touching persons bound to labor or involuntary service therein, nor to interfere with or abolish involuntary service in the District of Columbia without the consent of Maryland and without the consent of the owners, or making the owners who do not consent just compensation; nor the power to interfere with or prohibit representatives and others from bringing with them to the city of Washington, retaining and taking away, persons so bound to labor; nor the power to interfere with or abolish involuntary service in places under the exclusive jurisdiction of the United States within those States and Territories where the same is established or recognized; nor the power to prohibit the removal or transportation, by land, sea, or river, of persons held to labor or involuntary service in any State or Territory of the United States to any other State or Territory thereof where it is established or recognized by law or usage, and the right during transportation of touching at ports, shores, and landings, and of landing in case of distress, shall exist. Nor shall Congress have power to authorize any higher rate of taxation on persons bound to labor than on land.

SECTION 4. The third paragraph of the second section of the fourth article of the Constitution shall not be construed to prevent any of the States, by appropriate legislation, and through the action of their judicial and ministerial officers, from enforcing the delivery of fugitives from labor to the person to whom such service or labor is due.

SECTION 5. The foreign slave trade and the importation of slaves into the United States and their Territories, from places beyond the present limits thereof, are forever prohibited.

SECTION 6. The first, third, and fifth sections, together with this section six of these amendments, and the third paragraph of the second section of the first article of the Constitution, and the third paragraph of the second section of the fourth article thereof, shall not be amended or abolished without the consent of all the States.

SECTION 7. Congress shall provide by law that the United States shall pay to the owner the full value of his fugitive from labor, in all cases where the marshal, or other officer, whose duty it was to arrest such fugitive, was prevented from so doing by violence or intimidation from mobs or riotous assemblages, or when, after arrest, such fugitive was rescued by force, and the owner thereby prevented and obstructed in the pursuit of his remedy for the recovery of such fugitive.

FRANKFORT, March 20th, 1861.

To His Excellency, B. MAGOFFIN, Governor of Kentucky:

The undersigned, having made a brief report to you as Commissioners from the State of Kentucky, to the Convention of States assembled at Washington City, on the 4th of February last, on the invitation of the State of Virginia, and not having it in their power at that time to transmit a journal of their proceedings, beg leave now to do so. It came to hand to-day, and we avail ourselves of the earliest moment to submit it to your Excellency, and through you to the Legislature.

From this document it will be perceived that the Crittenden propositions, as modified by the suggestions of Virginia, were offered and failed to be passed. The original propositions of Mr. Crittenden were afterwards offered and likewise failed In both instances Kentucky voted as an unit in favor of the propositions. These having failed, the propositions heretofore transmitted to you were passed, and it may not be improper to give some explanations of the sections adopted.

The resolutions of Virginia suggested the amendments of the Constitution proposed by Mr. Crittenden, with additions proposed by that State, as the basis of the action of the Conference of States in their efforts to adopt some plan to restore harmony to a divided country and to preserve the Union. It will be proper here to state what were the leading provisions of Mr. Crittenden's proposed amendment, and also to state the amendment of the Constitution proposed by the Convention of States.

Upon the territorial question, the amendment of Mr. Crittenden provides, that "in all the territory now or hereafter to be acquired north of latitude 36 deg. 30 min., slavery or involuntary servitude, except as a punishment for crime, is prohibited; while in all territory south of that line slavery is hereby recognized as existing, and shall not be interfered with by Congress, but shall be protected as property by all the departments of the territorial government during its continuance; all the territory north or south of said line, within such boundaries as Congress may prescribe, when it contains a population necessary for a member of Congress, with a Republican form of goverment, shall be admitted into the Union on an equality with the original States, with or without slavery, as the Constitution of the State shall prescribe."

The corresponding section of the amendment proposed by the Conference of the States upon the same subject is as follows: "In all the present territory of the United States, north of the parallel of 36 deg. 30 min. north latitude, involuntary servitude, except as punishment of crimes, shall be prohibited. In all the present territories south of that line, the *status* of persons held to involuntary servitude or labor, as it now exists, shall not be changed; nor shall any law be passed by Congress or the territorial legislature to hinder or prevent the taking of such persons in the States of this Union to said territory, nor impair any rights arising from said relation; but the same shall be subject to the judicial cognizance of the Federal courts, according to the *course* of the common law;" the latter clause of which provides for the admission into the Union, in such convenient territory as Congress may provide, States with or without slavery, as their Constitution may provide, when the population shall be equal to the ratio of representation in Congress, shall be admitted into the Union. The only substantial difference between the two sections, that of Mr. Crittenden and the Convention of States, is, that the section of the Conference does not provide for a division of future acquired territory. This provision was objected to by many of the States represented, because they believed the present boundaries and territory of the United States were large enough; they did not wish to place in the Constitution a section which presented to the world that we were preparing our Government with power to make aggressions upon the territory of our neighbors.

It was believed that to insist upon this proposition, which may never be called into action, would prevent the harmonious settlement of the difficulties now existing between the two sections of the United States. We believe it would be regretted by every patriot if any honest and peaceful settlement of our present difficulties should be prevented, by insisting upon a provision dividing territory that the United States did not own, and may never acquire. With this exception, the proposition to divide the territory is the same in the amendment proposed by the Convention and by Mr. Crittenden's proposition. There is a difference of language, in some respects, between the two sections, but they both mean the same thing; that is, African slavery. The resolution of Mr. Crittenden declares that slavery or involuntary servitude shall not exist north of 36 deg. 30 min., while in all the territory south of that line, "slavery is hereby recognized as existing."

The section of the Conference employs the language of the present Constitution, the same language as is used in the ordinance of 1787 to express the same idea, which does mean, and has been held by the legislative, judicial, and executive departments of the Government to mean, African slavery and property in the same. The Representatives from the free States preferred the language employed in the Constitution, to which we could see no just objection; nor can there be any valid objection to the language employed in this section of the amendment.

The expressions used in Mr. Crittenden's section, "that slavery is hereby recognized as existing south of that line," was objected to by some, as it might be construed it meant to establish slavery in the territory by a constitutional provision. To obviate all difficulty, and remove all excuse for voting against this section of the Conference by those who manifested a desire to co-operate with the Southern States, the original proposition was amended in its language, and the section made to read, "that the *status* of persons held to involuntary service or labor, as it now exists, shall not be changed by any law of Congress or the territory."

It may be well here to state what is the *status* of persons held to involuntary service or labor in all the territory of the United States south of 36 deg. 30 min. By the law of New Mexico, which covers the whole of the territory south of that line, African slavery exists by territorial enactment, protected by the Constitution of the United States.

The laws of the Territory protect the right of the owner; provide remedies, civil and criminal, for injuries or violation of such right, as completely and as effectually as it is protected in the State of Kentucky. This right, as it now exists, and the right to take slaves into that territory, shall not be impaired or changed by Congress, or the laws of the territory. If, after the adoption of this clause as a part of the Constitution, the territorial legislature should repeal its laws, or there should be a change of the decision in the Dred Scott case, the right and interest of the master in his slave would not and could not be impaired.

It was thought by some that a territorial legislature might repeal the statutes furnishing the remedies now existing for the rights and protection of the owners of slaves, under the idea that it would not be a violation of the right or interest of the owner. The provision was added that the same—that is, the right in and to the slave, and for injuries—should be subject to the official cognizance of the Federal Courts, according to the course of the common law. It was believed that all intelligent minds, nay, any person of ordinary capacity, would comprehend the true meaning of this portion of the section. By some who are opposed to all adjustment of our present national difficulties, the meaning of this clause has been perverted. It is charged that the South has only secured to her such interest in African slavery as the common law recognizes; and as the common law does not recognize slavery in man, the provision is useless. Such objections do not discriminate between right and remedy. Slavery, as it now exists by law in New Mexico, is recognized, and is not to be impaired by law; and if the right be interfered with by others, if the territorial law has not furnished a remedy, the injured owner is remitted to that common law which provides an adequate remedy for every wrong committed upon person or property.

To charge that the section refers the master to the common law as giving or establishing his right to a slave, is an imputation upon the intelligence of the members of the Convention North and South, who voted for it. Take the clause as it stands, and the statute of New Mexico: if the clause were adopted as part of the Constitution, then we aver no owner of a slave in Kentucky is vested with a better right, or armed with a better remedy for the protection of that right and the redress of the injury committed upon his slave. The provision is better, it is more permanent for the protection of slave property in a territory, than the simple constitutional injunction, "that it shall be protected as property by all the departments of the territorial government."

The second section of the amendment proposed by the Conference is in these words: "No territory shall be acquired by the United States, except by discovery, and for naval and commercial stations, depots, and transit routes, without the concurrence of a majority of all the Senators, from the States which allow involuntary servitude, and from a majority of the Senators of the States which prohibit the relation. Nor shall territory be acquired by treaty, unless the votes of . of the Senators from each of the States hereinbefore mentioned be cast as a part of the two thirds majority necessary for the ratification of such treaty."

This section was proposed and insisted upon by Virginia, and was intended to qualify the treaty-making power of the United States, so as to secure each section against any improper annexation of territory ; and if such majority be obtained, it will be upon an agreement for a fair division between the two sections for settlement and occupation.

The third section of the article agreed to by the Convention is as follows :

" Neither the Constitution, nor any amendment thereof, shall be construed to give Congress the power to regulate, abolish, or control, within any State or Territory of the United States, the relation established and recognized by the laws thereof touching persons held to labor or involuntary service therein, nor to interfere with or abolish involuntary service in the District of Columbia, without the consent of Maryland, or without the consent of the owners, or making the owners who do not consent, just compensation ; nor the power to interfere with or prohibit Representatives or others from bringing with them to the District of Columbia, retaining and taking away, persons so held to labor or service ; nor the power to interfere with or abolish involuntary service in places under the exclusive jurisdiction of the United States, within those States and Territories where the same is established or recognized, nor the power to prohibit the removal or transportation of persons held to labor or involuntary service in any State or Territory of the United States, to any other State or Territory thereof, where it is established or recognized by law or usage ; and the right during the transportation, by sea or river, of touching at ports, shores, landings, and landing in case of distress, shall exist; but not the right of transit in or through any State or Territory for sale or traffic against the laws thereof; nor shall Congress have power to authorize any higher rate of taxation on persons held to labor or service, than lands. The bringing into the District of Columbia persons held to labor or service for sale, or placing them in depots, to be afterwards transferred to other places for sale as merchandise, is prohibited."

This section embraces all of the 2d, 3d, and 4th sections of Mr. Crittenden's amendment, except the latter clause, which proposed to guarantee the right to take slaves through States where slavery does not exist. The amendment of the Convention does not embrace this clause ; and the right to do so is left where it has always rested, to the comity of each State. Some of the States where slavery exists, have, by statutes, prohibited the passage or importation of slaves as merchandise, in or through their territory. They have prohibited the importation of slaves by their own citizens, for their own use, from other States. It was deemed that such a provision would be an invasion upon the rights of the States, and, therefore, the amendment of the Convention left that question where it has rested ever since the Constitution was adopted. The right thus to transport any slaves through any State is not embraced by the amendment. This exception applies to all the States, slave as well as free. The 4th section is as follows :

" The 3d paragraph of the 2d section of the 4th article of the Constitution shall not be construed to prevent any of the States, by appropriate legislation, and through the action of judicial and ministerial officers, from inforcing the delivery of fugitives from labor to persons to whom such labor is due."

It has been decided by the Supreme Court that any law of a State which provided means and furnished aid to the re-capture and return of fugitive slaves, was unconstitutional; this section permits States to pass such laws. The 5th section is as follows :

" The foreign slave trade is hereby forever prohibited, and it shall be the duty of Congress to pass laws to prevent the importation of slaves, coolies, or persons held to service or labor, into the United States and territories, from places beyond the limits thereof."

This section ought not to require any explanation ; no one can object to it except such as may desire the re-opening of the African slave trade. We have heard it suggested by some who seem to favor the independence of the seceded States, that upon their becoming independent and alien States, this clause would prohibit the importation of such slaves from these seceded States into the United States. This should be so, else the United States might have their territory flooded by the African race, whenever the Southern Confederacy shall open the African slave trade.

The 6th section prohibits the repeal of any of the guarantees in the Constitution, or in this amendment, in relation to slave property, without the consent of all the States.

The 7th section is as follows : Congress shall provide by law that the United States shall pay the owner full value for a fugitive from labor, in all cases where the marshal or other officer, whose duty it was to arrest such fugitive, was prevented from so doing by violence, or intimidation, from mobs or riotous assemblages, or when, after arrest, such fugitive was rescued by like violence or intimidation, and the owner thereby deprived of the same; and the acceptance of such payment shall preclude the owner from further claim to such fugitive. Congress shall provide by law for securing to citizens of each State the privileges and immunities of citizens in the several States.

This article is substantially the same as Mr. Crittenden's amendment. It makes it the duty of Congress to pay the owner the value of the slave, where the marshal shall be prevented by force or intimidation from executing the law, and where the slave shall be wrested from the owner after he is delivered. It was not necessary to provide in this section that Congress should provide by law how the United States may be indemnified for such payment. Under this clause, and the section of the Constitution upon the subject of fugitives from labor, the power to pass such laws for the indemnity of the United States against such wrong-doers is plenary and full.

The second section of ―― article of the Constitution of the United States now reads : " The citizens of each State shall enjoy the privileges and immunities of the citizens of the several States." It gave Congress no right to legislate upon the subject; it operates as a prohibition to each State from discriminating against the citizens of other

2

States, and would make void all such legislation. The clause added to the 7th section of this article, that Congress shall provide by law for securing to the citizens of each State the privileges and immunities of citizens in the several States, cannot do more than to make such discriminating laws void, and is therefore harmless.

The section of Mr. Crittenden's amendment giving power to Congress to acquire territory in Africa, or South America, for the colonization of free negroes, was not acceptable to the majority of the States. They seem to prefer to leave that question to the Colonization Society, as a subject better and cheaper managed than it would be under the Government of the United States. It is proper to state, that upon the 1st section of the amendment, the vote of the Commissioners of Kentucky was not unanimous, nor was it always so upon questions of amendments; but we claim for ourselves what we cheerfully accord to others, an honest and sincere purpose that some measure would be adopted that would give confidence, quiet, and security to the South; and we regret, that owing to the excited partisan state and condition of members of Congress, both North and South, the shortness of time permitted no fair test by a vote upon the amendment proposed.

Although the proposed amendment was not submitted to the States for adoption, the undersigned cannot hesitate to express a confident belief that the border free States would grant all the guarantees secured by the amendment, and they cannot believe that the remaining free States would refuse to do the same whenever the question shall be fairly presented to the people, which they hope may be done by the next Congress when it shall convene.

With great respect, yours, &c.,

C. A. WICKLIFFE,
JAMES GUTHRIE,
C. S. MOREHEAD,
JOSHUA F. BELL.

MINORITY REPORT.

To His Excellency, Beriah Magoffin, Governor of Kentucky:

The undersigned, two of the Commissioners appointed by resolution of the General Assembly of the Commonwealth of Kentucky, to meet such Commissioners as might be appointed by other States, in accordance with the request of the State of Virginia, to confer upon the unfortunate condition of our country, not having had an opportunity to unite with their co-commissioners in the report which they understand they have made, although they remained in the city of Washington a full day after the adjournment of the Convention for the purpose of joining with them in a proper report to your Excellency, feel it due to themselves, and respectful as well as due to the General Assembly, that they shall make this their separate report.

The undersigned felt themselves bound, for the guidance of their action in the Convention, to regard in some degree the 4th resolution of the General Assembly which they beg here to quote:

Resolved, That in the opinion of the General Assembly of Kentucky, the propositions embraced in the resolutions presented to the Senate of the United States, by the Hon. John J. Crittenden, so construed that the first article proposed as an amendment to the Constitution of the United States shall apply to all the Territory of the United States now held or hereafter acquired south of latitude 36 deg. and 30 min., and provide that slavery of the African race shall be effectually protected as property herein during the continuance of the territorial government; and the fourth article shall secure to the owners of slaves the right of transit with their slaves between and through the non-slaveholding States and Territories, constitute the basis of such an adjustment of the unhappy controversy which now divides the States of this Confederacy, as would be acceptable to the people of this Commonwealth.

They conceived that this resolution set forth clearly the opinion of the General Assembly, as to what adjustment would be acceptable to the people of Kentucky, and at the same time negatived the idea that the resolutions of Mr. Crittenden would be acceptable, unless construed in the manner set forth in the resolution. Whilst they did not consider it to give them positive instruction, they did not feel themselves to be at liberty to depart altogether from the wishes of the State, so solemnly announced by the representatives of its people.

The undersigned have delayed making their report until the present time, in the hope of being able to append to it, as a part thereof, the journal of the Convention, which would have shown every proposition made, with the vote by States upon such as were brought to a vote. They regret that although a committee was appointed for the express purpose of superintending the printing of said journal, they have not as yet received a copy of it, and that their report is more incomplete than they would have desired to have made it.

The Convention assembled in the city of Washington on the 4th of February, and continued its sessions until the 27th of that month, when it adjourned *sine die*. Before the final adoption of the proposed amendments to the Constitution, twenty-one States were present by their delegates in Convention. A Committee on Resolutions, consisting of a member from each State, was appointed, to whom was referred various propositions of adjustment. That committee finally reported, as the result of its deliberations, a proposition to amend the Constitution by a 13th article, consisting of 7 sections, a copy of which, marked A, is filed as a part hereof.

Notice of various substitutes for the report of the committee was given, but it was claimed and conceded that before a vote upon any substitute could be taken, the report of the committee should be amended and perfected in convention.

Many amendments were proposed; upon some of them, the undersigned were so unfortunate as to differ from the opinion of the majority of their co-commissioners who cast the vote of the State. To one or two of the more important of them they would briefly call attention. A motion was made by Gov. Reid, a delegate from North Carolina, to amend the 1st section of the series, by inserting at the end of the clause, "and in all the present territory south of said line," the words "*involuntary servitude is recognized, and property in those of the African race held to service or labor in any of the States of the Union, when removed to such territory, shall be protected and.*" This amendment received the votes of but three States—Virginia, North Carolina, and Missouri. Seventeen States voted against it, Kentucky being one of them. From this vote the undersigned caused their dissent to be recorded.

A motion was made by Mr. Seddon, a delegate from Virginia, to amend the 3d section of the series, by inserting at the end of the clause, "and the right during transportation of touching at ports, shores, and landings, and of landing in case of distress, shall exist," the words, "*and if the transportation shall be by sea, the right to persons held to service or labor shall be protected by the Federal Government as other property.*" This amendment was lost, Kentucky voting against it, from which vote the undersigned caused their dissent to be recorded.

The entire first section of the report of the committee was stricken out. In lieu thereof, a proposition made by Mr. Franklin, a delegate from Pennsylvania, was adopted. This proposition is the first section upon the paper marked B.

One of the undersigned (Mr. Clay) proposed, as an additional section to the report of the committee, a proposition to construe the second paragraph of the second section of the fourth article of the Constitution, so that no State shall have the power to judge and determine what was treason, felony, or other crime, by the laws of another State, but that a person charged with treason, felony, or other crime in one State, who should flee from justice and be found in another State, should, on demand of the Executive authority of the State from which he fled, be delivered up, to be removed to the State having jurisdiction of the crime. This amendment was lost; a large majority voting against it.

Amendments too numerous to set forth in the limits of a report, were offered and voted upon. Finally, the report of the committee was perfected, and is filed herewith as a part hereof, marked B.

Substitutes for the report of the committee, as amended and perfected, being now in order: among others, Mr. Seddon, of Virginia, offerred the amendments to the Constitution, known as the Crittenden resolutions, with such additions and amendments as were asked by Virginia, (in substance, the same as those set forth in the resolutions of the General Assembly of Kentucky.) This substitute v as rejected by a large majority—receiving the votes of only a few states.

One of the undersigned (Mr. Clay) then offered as a substitute for the report of the committee, the amendments to the Constitution, known as the Crittenden resolutions, without the crossing a "t" or dotting an "i." This substitute was rejected—16 States voting against it, and only 5 States voting for it.

All substitutes having been rejected, the perfected report of the committee (B) came up in order. Upon it, the vote of the convention was taken by sections. On the first vote upon the first section, it was rejected by the votes of 11 States to 8. The convention adjourned until the next morning ; when this vote was reconsidered.

The seven sections of the report were then passed by the convention.

Upon the first section, the vote stood, 9 States for, 8 States against. Four Southern States out of seven, and five Northern States out of fourteen, voting for it—Virginia and North Carolina both against it.

The second section was passed—11 States voting for it, 8 States against it.

The third section was passed—12 States voting for it, 7 States against it.

The fourth section was passed—15 States voting for it, 4 States against it.

The fifth section was passed—16 States voting for it, 5 States against it.

The sixth section was passed—11 States voting for it, 9 States against it.

The seventh section was passed—12 States voting for it, 7 States against it.

The vote of Kentucky was cast by the majority of her commissioners in favor of every section of the seven.

After the passage of the report by sections, a vote was demanded upon it as an entirety, but was ruled to be out of order.

The undersigned could not agree with their co-commissioners in casting the vote of Kentucky for the several sections of the proposed amendment to the Constitution, as adopted by the convention. They believed that the amendment, as a permanent settlement of the questions which have so unhappily divided the Northern and Southern sections of the United States, would prove wholly ineffectual, and that instead of providing securities and guarantees for the rights of the South, as they are believed now to exist under the Constitution and laws, involved a surrender of most important rights, and furnished adequate security to none. They propose to give briefly their reasons for this opinion.

The first section undertakes to settle the territorial question by dividing all the present territory of the United States by a line upon the parallel of 36 degrees 30 minutes, north latitude; and provides that north of that line involuntary servitude, except in punishment of crime, shall be prohibited; whilst south of that line the *status* of persons held to involuntary service or labor as it now exists, shall not be changed.

What is the present extent of the territory of the United States; and what is its *status* respecting persons held to involuntary service or labor?

The present territory of the United States, including 67,020 square miles held by the Cherokee Indians, under treaty grant, amounts to 1,287,277 square miles. By the southern construction of the decision of the Supreme Court, in the case of Dred Scott, into every foot of this vast territory persons held to involuntary service or labor may now be taken; and south of the line 36 degrees 30 minutes, the territorial law of New Mexico also permits it. The first section of the amendment proposes to take from the people of the South the right to carry persons held to involuntary service or labor into any of the territory north of 36 degrees 30 minutes; that is to say, forever to exclude such persons from 1,021,307 square miles of the territory of the United States; whilst it merely concedes the right, which they believe they already have as to the whole, to take such persons into 265,970 square miles of the territory—about one fourth of the whole. Would this be concession to the South, or to the North?

. But as to the *status* of the territory south of 36 degrees and 30 minutes, in respect to persons held to involuntary service or labor; what is it?

The right to take such persons into said territory rests, first, upon the decision of the Supreme Court in the Dred Scott case. Second, upon the territorial law of New Mexico, which territory embraces all south of 36 degrees and 30 minutes, except 50,290 square miles of the Cherokee treaty grant, where slavery now exists.

It is well known that a very large portion of the people of the North, as well as many of the South, maintain that the decision of the Supreme Court in the case of Dred Scott, so far as it relates to the question of slavery in the Territories, is no decision at all; simply *obiter dictu*, which does not settle the law upon the subject. That such is the opinion of the present Chief Magistrate is clear from his late inaugural. It is also avowed by the dominant party, that it is their intention to remodel the Supreme Court, and to have that decision reversed. If, then, the Dred Scott decision does not correctly declare the law, or if it be reversed, in either case, so far as the *status* of the Territory rests upon it, it would be free and not slave.

The Dred Scott case no longer to be relied on as fixing a *status* of slavery, we should be thrown altogether upon the territorial law of

New Mexico. But it is scarcely necessary to observe that a large portion of the American people believe that a Territorial Legislature has no power to pass laws either to introduce or to prohibit slavery in the Territories. Should the territorial law of New Mexico be hereafter decided to be void, the Dred Scott decision either no decision at all, or reversed, the *status* of even that small portion of the territory of the United States, 265,970 square miles out of 1,287,277 square miles, would be *free* and not slave.

What protection is proposed to be given to slave property south of the line 36 degrees and 30 minutes? The section merely provides, that neither Congress nor the Territorial Legislature shall pass any law to hinder or prevent the taking of persons held to involuntary service or labor to the Territory, nor to impair the rights arising from said relation; but the same (*the rights*) shall be subject to judicial cognizance in the Federal Courts, according to the course of the common law. What is the course of the common law in the remedies it affords to infringement upon the rights of property in slaves? Is it clear, unmistakable, not liable to misconstruction, especially when administered by judges unfriendly or adverse to the institution of slavery? Would the opinion, for example, of the distinguished Governor of New York, who now holds so high a place in the Cabinet, that a slave, not being a free man, could not under the common law be kidnapped, and that, therefore, there is no common law remedy for kidnapping a slave, be followed? Is this such protection for the right of property in the territories as Kentucky seeks as further security and further guarantee? How vain! How delusive! The proposition was but a miserable attempt to withdraw from the institution of slavery in the territories the protection of the Constitution and the Federal laws, and to have its only security to depend upon the vague and uncertain remedies of the common law.

If there had been no other objection to it, the first section of the amendment proposed by the Peace Conference, which received only the votes of four slave States out of seven, and five free States out of fourteen, was too doubtful in meaning, too liable to misconstruction—different constructions having been given to it even in the convention which passed it—to allow the undersigned, in justice to Kentucky, to vote for it as a measure of final adjustment.

The undersigned objected to the second section, because, crippling present rights, it rendered the future acquisition of any territory whatever—Cuba, or any other, no matter how important and desirable—almost impossible.

They objected to the third section because it failed to secure the right of transit, but left it in the power of any State or Territory to prevent the same. For example, placing it in the power of Illinois by Constitutional provision, if she chose to exercise it, to prevent the slaveholder of Kentucky from passing through that State with his slave property, on his way to Missouri or the South.

They objected to the 5th section, because, whether by constitutional right, or by revolutionary right, the so-called Southern Confederacy, being beyond the limits of the United States, or if not now beyond said limits, certainly to be so as soon as said Confederacy shall be recognized, it is made the duty of Congress, by the last clause of the section, to pass laws to prevent our friends and brothers, now residing within the limits of that Confederacy, from returning with their slaves to Kentucky ; the passage of which laws would inevitably lead to retaliatory laws by the Southern Confederacy against the introduction of slaves from Kentucky into their territory.

They objected to the 6th section, because it proposed to make the 1st, 3d, and 5th sections, amendments to the Constitution virtually unalterable.

They objected to the 7th section, because it proposed that any citizen of a slave State, who should lose his fugitive slave, by reason of mob, riotous assemblage, or rescue after arrest, should himself pay a part of his own loss, whilst every other citizen of a slave State should pay a part thereof, thus offering a bonus to deprive the people of the South of their property, and in effect by providing that the fugitive, having been thus paid for, shall thereafter be free, to constitute the United States government a grand Emancipation Society.

The undersigned have felt it to be proper thus to set forth the reasons which caused them to oppose the amendment to the Consti tution, which met the approval of the Peace Convention and of their co-Commissioners.

After the adoption of a preamble to the proposition of the Convention, the President was requested to cause the same to be presented to the two Houses of Congress, which was accordingly done, and its fate in that body is known to the country.

Before the final adjournment of the Convention, resolutions against the right of secession by a State from the Union, and in favor of such right, were proposed but not entertained. The following resolution was also proposed but not entertained by the Convention ; its mover, however, asked and obtained leave to have it spread upon the journal :

Resolved. That while the adoption, by the States of South Carolina, Georgia, Florida, Alabama, Mississippi, Louisiana, and Texas, of ordinances declaring the dissolution of their relations with the Union, is an event deeply to be deplored, and while abstaining from any judgment on their conduct, we would express the earnest hope that they may soon see cause to resume their honored places in this Confederacy of States ; yet to the end that such return may be facilitated, and from the conviction that the Union being formed by the assent of the people of the respective States, and being compatible only with freedom, and the republican institutions guaranteed to each, cannot and ought not to be maintained by force. we deprecate any effort by the Federal Government to coerce in any form the said States to reunion or submission, as tending to irreparable breach, and leading to incalculable ills ; and we earnestly invoke the abstinence from all counsels or measures of compulsion towards them.

In conclusion, the undersigned will only add, that as Commissioners to the Convention at Washington, they were actuated, throughout its entire deliberations, by the single and sole desire of being in some degree instrumental to the restoration of confidence between the divided sections of the country, and of bringing about a reconstruction of that once happy Union bequeathed to us by our fathers. They regret most sincerely to have to say that they have returned home with abated confidence and diminished hope of satisfactory adjustment.

Should the journal of the Convention be hereafter received, it will be forwarded to your Excellency, to be laid before the General Assembly.

The undersigned have the honor to be, with great respect,

Your obedient servants,

WILLIAM O. BUTLER,
JAMES B. CLAY, } *Commissioners.*

FRANKFORT, March 18th, 1861.

APPENDIX A.

REPORT OF COMMITTEE.—ARTICLE 13.

SECTION 1. In all the present territory of the United States, not embraced within the limits of the Cherokee treaty grant, north of a line from east to west on the parallel of 36 degrees 30 minutes north latitude, involuntary servitude, except in punishment of crime, is prohibited whilst it shall be under a Territorial government; and in all the present territory south of said line, the status of persons owing service or labor as it now exists shall not be changed by law while such territory shall be under a Territorial government; and neither Congress nor the Territorial government shall have power to hinder or prevent the taking to said territory of persons held to labor or involuntary service, within the United States, according to the laws or usages of the State from which such persons may be taken, nor to impair the rights arising out of said relations, which shall be subject to judicial cognizance in the federal courts, according to the common law; and when any territory north or south of said line, within such boundary as Congress may prescribe, shall contain a population required for a member of Congress, according to the then federal ratio of representation, it shall, if its form of government be republican, be admitted into the Union on an equal footing with the original States, with or without involuntary service or labor, as the constitution of such new State may provide.

SECTION 2. Territory shall not be acquired by the United States, unless by treaty; nor, except for naval and commercial stations and depots, unless such treaty shall be ratified by four fifths of all the members of the Senate.

SECTION 3. Neither the Constitution, nor any amendment thereof, shall be construed to give Congress power to regulate, abolish, or control, within any State or Territory of the United States, the relation established or recognized by the laws thereof touching persons bound to labor or involuntary service therein, nor to interfere with or abolish involuntary service in the District of Columbia without the consent of Maryland and without the consent of the owners, or making the owners who do not consent just compensation ; nor the power to interfere with or prohibit representatives and others from bringing with them to the city of Washington, retaining and taking away, persons so bound to labor; nor the power to interfere with or abolish involuntary service in places under the exclusive jurisdiction of the United States within those States and Territories where the same is established or recognized; nor the power to prohibit the removal or transportation, by land, sea, or river, of persons held to labor or involuntary service in any State or Territory of the United States to any other State or Territory thereof where it is established or recognized by law or usage, and the right during transportation of touching at ports, shores, and landings, and of landing in case of distress, shall exist. Nor shall Congress have power to authorize any higher rate of taxation on persons bound to labor than on land.

Section 4. The third paragraph of the second section of the fourth article of the Constitution shall not be construed to prevent any of the States, by appropriate legislation, and through the action of their judicial and ministerial officers, from enforcing the delivery of fugitives from labor to the person to whom such service or labor is due.

Section 5. The foreign slave trade and the importation of slaves into the United States and their Territories, from places beyond the present limits thereof, are forever prohibited.

Section 6. The first, third, and fifth sections, together with this section six of these amendments, and the third paragraph of the second section of the first article of the Constitution, and the third paragraph of the second section of the fourth article thereof, shall not be amended or abolished without the consent of all the States.

Section 7. Congress shall provide by law that the United States shall pay to the owner the full value of his fugitive from labor, in all cases where the marshal, or other officer, whose duty it was to arrest such fugitive, was prevented from so doing by violence or intimidation from mobs or riotous assemblages, or when, after arrest, such fugitive was rescued by force, and the owner thereby prevented and obstructed in the pursuit of his remedy for the recovery of such fugitive.

APPENDIX B.

REPORT OF COMMITTEE.—ARTICLE 13.

Section 1. In all the present territory of the United States, north of the parallel of 36 degrees and 30 minutes of north latitude, involuntary servitude, except in punishment of crime, is prohibited. In all the present territory south of that line, the status of persons held to involuntary service or labor, as it now exists, shall not be changed; nor shall any law be passed by Congress or the Territorial Legislature to hinder or prevent the taking of such persons from any of the States of this Union to said territory, nor to impair the rights arising from said relation; but the same shall be subject to judicial cognizance in the federal courts, according to the course of the common law. When any territory north or south of said line, within such boundary as

Congress may prescribe, shall contain a population equal to that required for a member of Congress, it shall, if its form of government be republican, be admitted into the Union on an equal footing with the original States, with or without involuntary servitude, as the constitution of such State may provide.

Section 2. No territory shall be acquired by the United States, except by discovery and for naval and commercial stations, depots, and transit routes, without the concurrence of a majority of all the Senators from States which allow involuntary servitude, and a majority of all the Senators from States which prohibit that relation; nor shall territory be acquired by treaty, unless the votes of a majority of the Senators from each class of States hereinbefore mentioned be cast as a part of the two-third majority necessary to the ratification of such treaty.

Section 3. Neither the Constitution, nor any amendment thereof, shall be construed to give Congress power to regulate, abolish, or control, within any State or Territory of the United States, the relation established or recognized by the laws thereof touching persons bound to labor or involuntary service therein, nor to interfere with or abolish involuntary service in the District of Columbia without the consent of Maryland and without the consent of the owners, or making the owners who do not consent just compensation; nor the power to interfere with or prohibit representatives and others from bringing with them to the city of Washington, retaining and taking away, persons so bound to labor or service; nor the power to interfere with or abolish involuntary service in places under the exclusive jurisdiction of the United States within those States and Territories where the same is established or recognized; nor the power to prohibit the removal or transportation of persons held to labor or involuntary service in any State or Territory of the United States to any other State or Territory thereof where it is established or recognized by law or usage; and the right during transportation, by sea or river, of touching at ports, shores, and landings, and of landing in case of distress, but not for sale or traffic, shall exist. Nor shall Congress have power to authorize any higher rate of taxation on persons held to labor or service than on land.

The bringing into the District of Columbia persons held to labor or' service for sale, or placing them in depots to be afterwards transferred to other places for sale as merchandise, is prohibited; and the right of transit through any State or Territory against its dissent is prohibited.

Section 4. The third paragraph of the second section of the fourth article of the Constitution shall not be construed to prevent any of the States, by appropriate legislation, and through the action of their judicial and ministerial officers, from enforcing the delivery of fugitives from labor to the person to whom such service or labor is due.

Section 5. The foreign slave trade is hereby forever prohibited; and it shall be the duty of Congress to pass laws to prevent the importation of slaves, coolies, or persons held to service or labor, into the United States and the Territories from places beyond the limits thereof.

SECTION 6. The first, third, and fifth sections, together with this section six of these amendments, and the third paragraph of the second section of the first article of the Constitution, and the third paragraph of the second section of the fourth article thereof, shall not be amended or abolished without the consent of all the States.

SECTION 7. Congress shall provide by law that the United States shall pay to the owner the full value of his fugitive from labor, in all cases where the marshal, or other officer, whose duty it was to arrest such fugitive, was prevented from so doing by violence or intimidation from mobs or riotous assemblages, or when, after arrest, such fugitive was rescued by like violence or intimidation, and the owner thereby prevented and obstructed in the pursuit of his remedy for the recovery of such fugitive; and the acceptance of such payment shall preclude the further claim of the owner. Congress shall provide by law for securing to the citizens of each State the privileges and immunities of the several States.

PROCEEDINGS

CONFERENCE CONVENTION.

WASHINGTON, *February 4th*, 1861.

A number of Commissioners assembled at Willards' Concert Hall, in consequence of the following preamble and resolutions adopted by the General Assembly of Virginia, January the 19th, 1861:

WHEREAS, It is the deliberate opinion of the General Assembly of Virginia, that unless the unhappy controversy, which now divides the States of this confederacy, shall be satisfactorily adjusted, a permanent dissolution of the Union is inevitable ; and the General Assembly, representing the wishes of the people of the Commonwealth, is desirous of employing every reasonable means to avert so dire a calamity, and determined to make a final effort to restore the Union and the Constitution, in the spirit in which they were established by the fathers of the Republic : therefore,

Resolved, That on behalf of the Commonwealth of Virginia, an invitation is hereby extended to all such States, whether slaveholding or non-slaveholding, as are willing to unite with Virginia in an earnest effort to adjust the present unhappy controversies, in the spirit in which the Constitution was originally formed, and consistently with its principles, so as to afford to the people of the slaveholding States adequate guarantees for the security of their rights, to appoint commissioners to meet on the 4th day of February next, in the City of Washington, similar commissioners appointed by Virginia, to consider, and if practicable, agree upon some suitable adjustment.

Resolved, That ex-President John Tyler, William C. Rives, Judge John W. Brockenbrough, George W. Summers, and James A. Seddon, are hereby appointed commissioners, whose duty it shall be to repair to the City of Washington, on the day designated in the foregoing resolution, to meet such commissioners as may be appointed by any of the said States, in accordance with the foregoing resolution.

Resolved, That if said commissioners, after full and free conference, shall agree upon any plan of adjustment requiring amendments to the Federal Constitution, for the further security of the rights of the people of the slaveholding States, they be requested to communicate the proposed amendments to Congress, for the purpose of having the same submitted by that body, according to the forms of the Constitution, to the several States for ratification.

Resolved, That if said commissioners cannot agree on such adjustment, or if agreeing, Congress shall refuse to submit for ratification such amendments as may be proposed, then the commissioners of this State shall immediately communicate the result to the executive of this Commonwealth, to be by him laid before the convention of the people of Virginia and the General Assembly : provided, that the said commissioners be subject at all times to the control of the General Assembly, or, if in session, to that of the State Convention.

Resolved, That in the opinion of the General Assembly of Virginia, the propositions embraced in the resolutions presented to the Senate of the United States by the Hon. John J. Crittenden, so modified as that the first article proposed as an amendment to the Constitution of the United States shall apply to all the territory of the United States now held, or hereafter acquired, South of latitude thirty-six degrees and thirty minutes, and provide that slavery of the African race shall be effectually protected as property therein during the continuance of the territorial government, and the fourth article shall secure to the owners of slaves the right of transit with their slaves between and through the non-slaveholding States and Territories, constitute the basis of such an adjustment of the unhappy controversy which now divides the States of this confederacy, as would be accepted by the people of this Commonwealth.

Resolved, That ex-President John Tyler is hereby appointed, by the concurrent vote of each branch of the General Assembly, a commissioner to the President of the United States, and Judge John Robertson is hereby appointed, by a like vote, a commissioner to the State of South Carolina, and the other States that have seceded or shall secede, with instructions respectfully to request the President of the United States, and authorities of such States, to agree to abstain, pending the proceedings contemplated by the action of this General Assembly, from any and all acts calculated to produce a collision of arms between the States and the Government of the United States.

Resolved, That copies of the foregoing resolutions be forthwith telegraphed to the executives of the several States, and also to the President of the United States, and the Governor be requested to inform, without delay, the commissioners of their appointment by the foregoing resolutions.

A copy from the rolls.

WM. F. GORDON, Jr.,
C. H. D. & K. R. of Va.

Mr. Morehead, of Kentucky, called the meeting to order, and moved that Mr. J. C. Wright, of Ohio, be appointed temporary chairman; to be followed by the appointment of a committee, consisting of a member from each delegation, to be named by such delegation, who should recommend officers for a permanent organization, and should also report rules for the government of the body.

The motion to appoint Mr. Wright was thereupon put and unanimously carried.

Upon being conducted to the chair by Mr. Meredith, of Pennsylvania, and Mr. Chase, of Ohio, Mr. Wright made a brief address explanatory of the object of the meeting, and expressed a hope and belief, that, as the delegates present from the several States had assembled under the influence of the most friendly feelings, if they carried those feelings into an examination of the difficulties which surround the country, the result would be a success, earnestly to be hoped for by every lover of his country, so as to establish the Union, according to the spirit of the existing Constitution of the United States.

On motion, Mr. Benjamin C. Howard, of Maryland, was appointed Secretary.

The following States responded to the call of their names—the list of delegates to be handed in to-morrow:

New Hampshire, Rhode Island, New Jersey, Pennsylvania, Delaware, Maryland, Virginia, North Carolina, Kentucky, Ohio, and Indiana.

Mr. Meredith, of Pennsylvania, then renewed the motion for the appointment of a committee as above mentioned, which was carried, and the following members named by their respective delegations, viz:

New Hampshire, Amos Tuck; Rhode Island, William W. Hoppin; New Jersey, Joseph F. Randolph; Pennsylvania, Thomas E. Franklin; Delaware, George B. Rodney; Maryland, John W. Crisfield; Virginia, William C. Rives; North Carolina, Thomas Ruffin; Kentucky, Charles A. Wickliffe; Ohio, Reuben Hitchcock; Indiana, Godlove S. Orth.

On motion, the Convention adjourned until to-morrow, at twelve o'clock.

B. C. HOWARD, *Secretary.*

WASHINGTON CITY, *February* 5, 1861.

The Convention was called to order pursuant to adjournment, by Mr. Wright, President *pro tem.*

The journal of proceedings of yesterday was read and approved.

Mr. Thomas E. Franklin, of Pennsylvania, moved that a committee of five be appointed by the President, to whom the credentials of members should be submitted and reported on, which was carried.

The President thereupon appointed as said committee:

Mr. Summers, of Virginia.

Mr. Guthrie, of Kentucky.

Mr. Morehead, of North Carolina.

Mr. Smith, of Indiana.

Mr. Franklin, of Pennsylvania.

Mr. Wickliffe, of Kentucky, from the Committee on Organization, made a report, which was read.

Mr. Clay, of Kentucky, moved to strike out for the present, and for further consideration, the report which relates to the proceedings of the Convention.

This motion gave rise to a debate, pending which a division of the report was called for; whereupon it was moved that the Convention proceed to consider the following part of the report of the committee, relating to officers for the permanent organization of the Convention, as follows:

The committee to whom was referred the subject of the organization of the Convention make the following report: They recommend that the permanent officers of the Convention be a President and Secretary, and that the Secretary have leave to appoint assistants, not exceeding two, to assist him in the discharge of his duties. The committee report, for President, John Tyler, of Virginia; Secretary, Crafts J. Wright, of Ohio.

Thereupon it was moved and unanimously agreed, that this part of the report be accepted, and the officers designated be appointed.

The President *pro tem.* appointed Mr. Ewing, of Ohio, and Mr. Meredith, of Pennsylvania, to conduct President Tyler to the chair.

President Tyler, on taking his seat, proceeded to address the Convention:

GENTLEMEN: I fear you have committed a great error in appointing me to the honorable position you have assigned me. A long separation from all deliberative bodies has rendered the rules of their proceedings unfamiliar to me, while I should find in my own state of health, variable and fickle as it is, sufficient reason to decline the honor of being your presiding officer. But, in times like these, one has but little option left him. Personal considerations should weigh but lightly in the balance. The country is in danger; it is enough. One must take the place assigned him in the great work of reconciliation and adjustment.

The voice of Virginia has invited her co-States to meet her in council. In the initiation of this Government that same voice was heard and complied with, and the results of seventy odd years have fully attested the wisdom of the decisions then adopted. Is the urgency of her call now less great than it was then? Our godlike fathers created; we have to preserve. They built up through their wisdom and patriotism monuments which have eternized their names. You have before you, gentlemen, a task equally grand, equally sublime, quite as full of glory and immortality. You have to snatch from ruin a great and glorious Confederacy, to preserve the Government, and to renew and invigorate the Constitution. If you reach the height of this great occasion your children's children will rise up and call you blessed. I confess myself to be ambitious of sharing in the glory of accomplishing this grand and magnificent result. To have our names enrolled in the capitol, to be repeated by future generations with grateful applause, this is an honor higher than the mountains, more enduring than the monumental alabaster.

Yes, Virginia's voice, as in the olden time, has been heard. Her sister States meet her this day at the council board. Vermont is here, bringing with her the memories of the past, and reviving in the memories of all her Ethan Allen and his demand for the surrender of Ticonderoga in the name of the Great Jehovah and the American Congress. New Hampshire is here, her fame illustrated by memorable annals, and still more lately as the birth-place of him who won for himself the name of Defender of the Constitution, and who wrote that letter to John Taylor which has been enshrined in the hearts of his countrymen. Massachusetts is not here. [Some member said she is coming.] I hope so, said Mr. Tyler, and that she will bring with her her daughter, Maine. I did not believe it could well be that the voice which in other times was so familiar to her ears had been addressed to her in vain. Connecticut is here, and she comes, I doubt not, in the spirit of Roger Sherman, whose name with our very children has become a household word, and who was in life the embodiment of that sound practical sense which befits the great lawgiver and constructor of governments. Rhode Island, the land of Roger Williams, is here, one of the two last States, in her jealousy of the public liberty, to give in her adhesion to the Constitution, and among the earliest to hasten to its rescue. The great Empire State of New York, represented thus far but by one delegate, is expected daily in fuller force to join in the great work of healing the discontents of the times and restoring the reign of fraternal feeling. New Jersey is also here, with the memories of the past covering her all over. Trenton and Princeton live immortal in story, the plains of the last encrimsoned with the heart's blood of Virginia's sons. Among her delegation I rejoice to recognize a gallant son of a signer of the immortal Declaration which announced to the world that thirteen Provinces had become thirteen independent and sovereign States. And here, too, is Delaware, the land of the Bayards and the Rodneys, whose soil at Brandywine was moistened by the blood of Virginia's youthful Monroe. Here is Maryland, whose massive columns wheeled into line with those of Virginia in the contest for glory, and whose State-house at Annapolis was the theater of a spectacle of a successful commander, who, after liberating his country, gladly ungirthed his sword and laid it down upon the altar of that country. Then comes Pennsylvania, rich in Revolutionary lore, bringing with her the deathless names of Franklin and Morris, and I trust ready to renew from the belfry of Independence Hall the chimes of the old bell which announced freedom and independence in former days. All hail to North Carolina, with her Mecklenburg Declaration in her hand, standing erect on the ground of her probity and firmness in the cause of the public liberty, and represented in her attributes by her Macon, and in this assembly by her distinguished son at no great distance from me. Four daughters of Virginia also cluster around the council board on the invitation of their ancient mother—the eldest Kentucky, whose sons, under the intrepid warrior, Anthony Wayne, gave freedom of settlement to the territory of her sister Ohio. She extends her hand daily and hourly across *la belle riviere*, to grasp the hand of some one of kindred blood of the noble States of Indiana, and Illinois, and Ohio, who have grown up into powerful States, already grand, potent, and almost imperial. Tennessee is not here, but is coming—prevented from being here only by the floods which have swollen her rivers. When she arrives she will wear the badges on her warrior crest of victories won, in company with the great West, on many an ensanguined plain, and standards torn from the hands of the conquerors at Waterloo. Missouri and Iowa, and Michigan, Wisconsin, and Minnesota, still linger behind, but it may be hoped that their hearts are with us in the great work we have to do.

Gentlemen, the eyes of the whole country are turned to this assembly in expectation and hope. I trust that you may prove yourselves worthy of the great occasion. Our ancestors probably committed a blunder in not having fixed upon every fifth decade for a call of a General Convention to amend and reform the Constitution. On the contrary, they have made the difficulties next to insurmountable to accomplish amendments to an instrument which was perfect for five millions of people, but not wholly so as to thirty millions. Your patriotism will surmount the difficulties, however great, if you will but accomplish but one triumph in advance, and that is, a triumph over party. And what is party when compared to the task of rescuing one's country from danger? Do that, and one long, loud shout of joy and gladness will resound throughout the land.

On motion of Mr. Ewing, action on the remainder of the report of the committee on organization was postponed until Wednesday.

Mr. Wickliffe, of Kentucky, offered the following resolution:

Resolved, That the Convention shall be opened with prayer, and that the clergy of the City of Washington be requested to perform that service.

Which was adopted; and at the request of the Convention, the Rev. Dr. Gurley offered up prayer.

The Convention being informed by the President of the tender by the Mayor and Council of the City of Washington of police officers to attend the sittings of the Convention, and protect the same from intrusion; and also that the hall now occupied had been placed at the service of the Convention; it was moved and agreed to, that the same be accepted.

On motion of Mr. Johnson, of Maryland, it was resolved that the President be requested to furnish a copy of his speech to the Convention to be made part of this day's proceedings, and that the same shall with the proceedings of this day be published.

Mr. Grimes, of Iowa, informed the Convention that he had a letter in regard to the appointment of delegates from Iowa, which was referred to the Committee on Credentials.

On motion of Mr. Wright, of Ohio, the Convention adjourned until 12 o'clock to-morrow.

———

WASHINGTON, *February 6th*, 1861.

The Convention met pursuant to adjournment.

President Tyler in the chair.

The journal of the proceedings of yesterday was read, amended, and approved.

Mr. Summers, chairman of the Committee on Credentials, made the following report:

The credentials of the following gentlemen from the States hereafter enumerated, have been duly submitted and examined by your committee, and approved by them, and they were reported as members of the Convention:

New Hampshire—Amos Tuck, Levi Chamberlain, Asa Fowler.

Vermont—Hiland Hall, Levi Underwood, H. Henry Baxter, L. E. Chittenden, B. D. Harris.

Rhode Island and Providence Plantations—Samuel Ames, Alexander Duncan, William W. Hoppin, George H. Browne, Samuel G. Arnold.

Connecticut—Roger S. Baldwin. Chauncey F. Cleveland, Charles J. McCurdy, James T. Pratt, Robbins Battell, Amos S. Treat.

New Jersey—Charles S. Olden, Peter D. Vroom, Robert F. Stockton, Benjamin Williamson, Joseph F. Randolph, Frederick T. Frelinghuysen, Rodman M. Price, William C. Alexander, Thomas J. Stryker.

Pennsylvania—James Pollock, William M. Meredith, Thomas White, David Wilmot, A. W. Loomis, Thomas E. Franklin, William McKennan.

Delaware—George B. Rodney, Daniel M. Bates, Henry Ridgely, John W. Houston, William Cannon.

Maryland—John F. Dent, Reverdy Johnson, John W. Crisfield, Augustus W. Bradford, William T. Goldsborough, J. Dixon Roman, Benjamin C. Howard.

Virginia—John Tyler, William C. Rives, John W. Brockenbrough, George W. Summers, James A. Seddon.

North Carolina—George Davis, Thomas Ruffin, David S. Reid, D. M. Barringer, J. M. Morehead.

Kentucky—William O. Butler, James B. Clay, Joshua F. Bell, Charles S. Morehead, James Guthrie, Charles A. Wickliffe.

Ohio—John C. Wright, Salmon P. Chase, William S. Groesbeck, Franklin T. Backus, Reuben Hitchcock, Thomas Ewing, V. B. Horton.

Indiana—Caleb B. Smith, Pleasant A. Hackleman, Godlove S. Orth, E. W. H. Ellis, Thomas C. Slaughter.

Iowa—James Harlan, James W. Grimes, Samuel H. Curtis, William Vandever.

On motion of Mr. Wickliffe, the Secretary was authorized to employ additional assistants.

Mr. Wickliffe, chairman of the Committee on Organization, called up for consideration that part of the report not heretofore agreed to, and moved that the same be adopted.

4

Mr. Seddon, of Virginia, offered the following amendment:

Resolved, That no part of the Journal be published without the order or leave of the Convention, and that no copies of the whole or any part be furnished or allowed, except to members, who shall be privileged to communicate the same to the authorities or deliberative assemblies of their respective States, when deemed judicious or appropriate under their instructions, and that nothing spoken in the house be printed or otherwise published; but private communications respecting the proceedings and debates, while recommended to be with caution and reserve, are allowed at the discretion of each member.

On motion, the above resolution and the original report and resolution, were referred back to the committee.

Mr. Guthrie, of Kentucky, moved the adoption of the following resolution :

Resolved, That a committee of one from each State be appointed by the Commissioners thereof, to be nominated to the President, and to be appointed by him, to whom shall be referred the resolutions of the State of Virginia, and the other States represented, and all propositions for the adjustment of existing difficulties between States, with authority to report what they may deem right, necessary, and proper to restore harmony and preserve the Union, and that they report on or before Friday.

Mr. Ewing, of Ohio, suggested that the resolution be so modified as to authorize said committee to sit during the meeting of the Convention; which being accepted, the resolution was agreed to.

The President appointed the following committee to carry into effect that part of the report of the Committee on Rules and Organization, which related to obtaining the services of a clergyman to open the proceedings with prayer:

Mr. Randolph, of New Jersey; Mr. Wickliffe, of Kentucky; Mr. Johnson, of Maryland.

On motion of Mr. Johnson, of Maryland, it was agreed that the members of this Convention should call in a body on the President of the United States at such time as would be agreeable to him, to be announced by the President of this Convention.

On motion, the Convention reconsidered the resolution recommitting the rules of proceeding to the committee thereon, and agreed to proceed to the consideration of the same.

Mr. Wright called for a division, and proposed that the several rules should be separately read, and, when no objection was raised, they should be agreed to; and when objected to, should be passed for subsequent consideration.

Which was agreed to.

The rules hereafter designated were adopted.

The remainder were recommitted.

The rules adopted were as follows:

1. A Convention to do business shall consist of the Commissioners of not less than seven States; and all questions shall be decided by the greater number of those which be fully represented. But a less number than seven may adjourn from day to day.

2. Immediately after the President shall have taken the chair, and the members their seats, the minutes of the preceding day shall be read by the Secretary.

3. Every member rising to speak shall address the President, and while he shall be speaking none shall pass between them, or hold discourse with another, or read a book, pamphlet, or paper, printed or manuscript—and of two members rising to speak at the same time, the President shall name him who shall be first heard.

4. A member shall not speak oftener than twice, without special leave, upon the same question, and not a second time, before every other who had been silent shall have been heard, if he choose to speak upon the subject.

5. A motion made and seconded, shall be repeated, and if written, as it shall be when any member shall so require, read aloud, by the Secretary, before it shall be debated—and may be withdrawn at any time before the vote upon it shall have been declared.

6. Orders of the day shall be read next after the minutes, and either discussed or postponed, before any other business shall be introduced.

7. When a debate shall arise upon a question, no motion, other than to amend the question to commit it, or to postpone the debate, shall be received.

8. A question which is complicated shall, at the request of any member, be divided and put separately upon the proposition of which it is compounded.

9. A writing which contains any matter brought on to be considered, shall be read once throughout, for information, then by paragraphs, to be debated, and again with the amendments, if any made on the second reading, and afterwards the question shall be put upon the whole, as amended, or approved in the original form, as the case may be.

10. Committees shall be appointed by the President, unless otherwise ordered by the Convention.

11. A member may be called to order by any other member, as well as by the President, and may be allowed to explain his conduct or expressions, supposed to be reprehensible. And all questions of order shall be decided by the President, without appeal or debate.

12. Upon a question to adjourn for the day, which may be made at any time, if it be seconded, the question shall be put without debate.

13. When the Convention shall adjourn, every member shall stand in his place until the President pass him.

14. That no member be absent from the Convention, so as to interrupt the representation of the State, without leave.

15. That committees do not sit while the Convention shall be or ought to be sitting, without leave of the Convention.

16. That no copy be taken of any entry on the Journal, during the sitting of the Convention, without leave of the Convention.

17. That members only be permitted to inspect the Journal.

18. Mode of voting: All votes shall be taken by States, and each State to give one vote. The yeas and nays of the members shall not be taken or published—only the decision by States.

On motion, the Convention adjourned until Thursday, 10 o'clock, A. M.

WASHINGTON CITY, *February 7th.* 1861.

The Convention met pursuant to adjournment.

President Tyler in the chair.

The Convention was opened by prayer by Rev. Dr. Pyne.

The journal of the proceedings of the Convention of the 6th instant was read, amended, and approved.

President Tyler, in accordance with the resolution of the 6th instant, in regard to calling on the President of the United States, caused to be read by the Secretary the following letter:

FEBRUARY 6th, 1861.

My DEAR SIR: I shall feel greatly honored to receive the gentlemen composing the Convention of Commissioners from the several States, on any day and at any hour most convenient to themselves. I shall name to-morrow, Thursday, at 11 or 3 o'clock, though any other time would be equally agreeable to me. I shall at all times be prepared to give them a cordial welcome.

Yours, very respectfully, JAMES BUCHANAN.
His Excellency, JOHN TYLER.

President Tyler asked the action of the Convention on the subject.

On motion of Mr. Guthrie, it was

Resolved, That the members of the Convention call on the President of the United States this forenoon, at 11 o'clock.

Mr. Summers, from the Committee on Credentials, reported that the credentials of the following gentlemen from the States hereafter enumerated, had been duly submitted and examined, and were approved by them; and approved as members of the Convention:

New York—William E. Dodge.

Tennessee—Samuel Milligan, Josiah M. Anderson, Robert L. Caruthers, Thomas Martin, Isaac R. Hawkins, R. J. McKinney, Alvin Cullom, Wm.

P. Hickerson, George W. Jones, F. K. Zollicoffer, William H. Stephens, A. O. W. Totten.

Illinois—John Wood, Stephen T. Logan, John M. Palmer, Burton C. Cook. Thomas J. Turner.

Which report was accepted.

Mr. Wickliffe, from the Committee on Organization, offered the following resolution:

Resolved, That the Secretary procure for the use of the Convention the necessary stationery; and also provide for such printing as may be ordered. That the Journal up to and including this day's proceedings, as well as the Rules, be printed for the use of the members. .

Which was passed.

The President appointed the following gentlemen members of the committee on Mr. Guthrie's resolution of yesterday:

New Hampshire, Asa Fowler; *Vermont*, Hiland Hall; *Rhode Island and Providence Plantations*, Samuel Ames; *Connecticut*, Roger S. Baldwin; *New Jersey*, Peter D. Vroom; *Pennsylvania*, Thomas White; *Delaware*, Daniel M. Bates; *North Carolina*, Thomas Ruffin; *Kentucky*, James Guthrie; *Ohio*, Thomas Ewing; *Indiana*, Caleb B. Smith; *Illinois*, Stephen T. Logan; *Iowa*, James Harlan; *Maryland*, Reverdy Johnson; *Virginia*, James A. Seddon.

Mr. Wickliffe, from the Committee on Organization, reported the following:

20th Rule. That nothing spoken in the Convention be printed or otherwise published or communicated without leave.

Which was agreed to.

Convention then adjourned.

———

WASHINGTON CITY, *February 8*, 1861.

The Convention met pursuant to adjournment.

President Tyler in the chair.

The Convention was opened with prayer by the Rev. Dr. Butler.

The journal of yesterday was read, amended, and approved.

Mr. Summers, from the Committee on Credentials, made report that the credentials of the gentlemen hereafter named, and from the States designated, had been duly submitted, examined, and approved as members of the Convention:

Massachusetts.—John Z. Goodrich, John M. Forbes, Richard P. Waters, Theophilus P. Chandler, Francis B. Crowninshield, George S. Boutwell, Charles Allen.

New York.—David Dudley Field, William Curtis Noyes, James S. Wadsworth, James C. Smith, Amaziah B. James, Erastus Corning, Addison Gardiner, Greene C. Bronson, John A. King, John E. Wool.

Missouri.—John D. Coalter, Alexander M. Doniphan, Waldo P. Johnson, Aylett H. Buckner, Harrison Hough.

The President appointed the following additional members of the committee on Mr. Guthrie's resolution: A. M. Doniphan, of Missouri; F. K. Zollicoffer, of Tennessee; David Dudley Field, of New York.

Mr. Guthrie, of Kentucky, informed the Convention that the committee of which he was chairman could not make report this day, according to order, and asked further time.

Mr. Clay, of Kentucky, moved that the committee have until Monday next to report. That delegates who should arrive from States not heretofore reported, might present their credentials to the committee thereon, and, being accepted, might select and report a member of Mr. Guthrie's committee through the Secretary to said committee; which motion was agreed to.

On motion of Mr. Ellis, of Indiana, it was

Ordered, That for the purpose of relieving the Doorkeeper from embarrassment, the President be requested to issue cards of admission to the members and officers of this Convention.

Mr. Hitchcock, of Ohio, asked of the President his interpretation of the rule of the Convention, heretofore adopted, in regard to the degree of secrecy required.

The President informed the Convention that, by his interpretation of the rules, nothing which was said or done in the Convention, in reference to any subject before it, could be spoken of, or divulged to, any but members.

Adjourned to Saturday, at 12 o'clock.

WASHINGTON CITY, *February* 9, 1861.

Convention met pursuant to adjournment.

President Tyler in the chair.

The Convention was opened by prayer from the Rev. Dr. Bullock, of Kentucky.

The journal of yesterday was read, amended, and approved.

Mr. Summers, from the Committee on Credentials, reported that the credentials from the gentlemen hereafter named had been duly submitted to them, examined, and approved, and they were reported by said committee as delegates from the States designated, viz:

Maine.—William P. Fessenden, Lot M. Morrell, Daniel E. Somes, John J. Perry, Ezra B. French, Freeman H. Morse, Stephen Coburn, Stephen C. Foster.

The following gentlemen were announced as additional members of the committee on Mr. Guthrie's resolution:

Francis B. Crowninshield, Massachusetts.

Lot M. Morrell, Maine.

Mr. Tuck, of New Hampshire, offered for consideration certain resolutions; which were read, and referred to the Committee on Resolutions.

Mr. Clay, of Kentucky, presented certain resolutions from Connecticut, and moved their reference to the Committee on Resolutions; which was agreed to.

On motion of Mr. Randolph, the Secretary was authorized to publish and furnish, for the use of members, a list of delegates to, and officers of, this Convention.

Convention adjourned until Monday, at 12 o'clock.

WASHINGTON CITY, *February* 11, 1861.

The Convention met pursuant to adjournment.

President Tyler in the chair.

The Convention was opened with prayer by the Rev. Dr. Gurley.

The journal of proceedings of Saturday was read, amended, and approved.

Mr. Guthrie, from the Committee on Resolutions, asked for further time to made report; which was given.

Mr. Guthrie, from the same committee, to whom were referred certain resolutions from Connecticut, made the following report:

The committee to whom were referred certain resolutions of the Democratic party of the State of Connecticut, report that, in the opinion of the committee, it is inexpedient for this Convention to act upon any resolution purporting to emanate from any political party whatever, and that the member of the Convention by whom the same were presented have leave to withdraw the same.

The President announced to the Convention that cards of admission for the members of the Convention upon the floor of the House of Representatives had been sent to him by the Door-keeper, and which the Secretary would deliver to the members who would call for them.

On motion of Mr. Chase, it was resolved that any propositions or resolutions which any member desired to have considered, and which under the rule passed to the Committee on Resolutions and Propositions, might be presented to said committee through the Secretary, without being presented in Convention.

Convention adjourned until Wednesday next, 12 o'clock.

WASHINGTON CITY, *February* 13, 1861.

The Convention met pursuant to adjournment.

President Tyler in the chair.

The Convention was opened with prayer by the Rev. Dr. Edwards.

The journal of Monday was read, amended, and approved.

Mr. Guthrie, from the Committee on Resolutions and Propositions, asked until Friday to make report.

Agreed to.

Mr. Seddon, of Virginia, asked permission of the Convention to communicate to the authorities of Virginia the state of proceedings in Convention and Committee.

Mr. Barringer, of North Carolina, offered the following:

Resolved, That the Commissioners of any State represented in this Convention, upon their joint application, have leave to communicate to the Legislature, Governor, or Convention of said State, the proceedings of this body, or so much thereof as they may deem expedient.

Which being seconded and accepted by Mr. Seddon,

Mr. Frelinghuysen, of New Jersey, moved to amend said resolution by adding thereto:

But not to communicate what has transpired in the Committee, before said Committee has reported to the Convention.

On motion of Mr. Seddon, the amendment and the resolution were laid on the table, subject to call after Friday.

Convention adjourned to Friday, 12 o'clock.

WASHINGTON CITY, *February* 14th, 1861.

The Convention met in special session, pursuant to the call of the President.

The proceedings were opened with prayer by the Rev. Dr. Hall.

The following letter from the Secretary, Crafts J. Wright, was read, and ordered to be entered upon the minutes:

WILLIARDS' HOTEL, WASHINGTON CITY, }
February 13th, 1861. }

Hon. JOHN TYLER, *President of Conference Convention:*

DEAR SIR : I grieve to communicate to you the fact that the delegate from Ohio to this Conference Convention, the Hon. John C. Wright, departed this life this day, the 13th of February, at half-past one o'clock.

Judge Wright came to this Convention with a heart filled with fear for the safety of the Union. Though at an advanced age, and nearly blind, he was filled with an earnest desire to add his efforts to that of others of the Convention called by the State of Virginia, and seek to agree on some measures, honorable to each and all, to effect the object. Since the arrival of my father in Washington, he has been constant in his efforts to effect the end in view, and he has had his heart cheered with the belief that the object would be accomplished. Almost the last words he uttered were, that he believed the Union would be preserved. He desired me to say, if the Union was saved, he would die content. He called me to read to him at twelve o'clock, the sections in the Constitution in regard to counting the votes, and this request, and this reading, terminated his knowledge on earth.

In this desire of my father to do what he could, he pressed me to accompany him on account of his blindness. Since the Convention honored me with the appointment of Secretary, he required of me a promise that I would not leave the position. When I read the section of the Constitution to him, he required me then to leave him for the Convention. Whatever my personal feelings may be, I deem the pledge made sacred. I therefore ask that I may have leave of absence, until I carry the remains home to Ohio and return to my duty.

Respectfully, CRAFTS J. WRIGHT.

P. S.—J. Henry Puleston will act for me in my absence.

The President informed the Convention that the request of the Secretary had been complied with.

The President asked what action the Convention proposed to take on the subject for which they had been specially assembled.

The Hon. Salmon P. Chase, of Ohio, then said :

Mr. President, since we assembled yesterday in this Hall it has pleased God to remove one of our number from all participation in the concerns of earth. It is my painful duty to announce to the Convention that JOHN C. WRIGHT, one of the Commissioners from Ohio, is no more. Full of years, honored by the confidence of the people, rich in large experience and ripened wisdom, and devoted in all his affections and all his powers to his country, and his whole country, he has been called from our midst at the very moment when the prudence and patriotism of his counsels seemed most needed. Such are the mysterious ways of Divine Providence !

Judge Wright was born in Wethersfield, Connecticut, on the 10th of August, 1784. The death of his parents made him an orphan in infancy; and he had little to depend upon in youth and early manhood, save his own energies and God's blessing.

He was married, while young, to a daughter of Thomas Collier, of Litchfield, and for several years after resided at Troy, New York.

When about twenty-six years old, he removed to Steubenville, in Ohio, where he commenced the practice of the law, and rapidly rose to distinction in the profession.

In 1822, he was elected a Representative in Congress, where he became the associate and friend of Clay and of Webster, and proved himself, on many occasions, worthy of their association and friendship.

After serving several terms in Congress, he was elected a Judge of the Supreme Court of Ohio, and, in 1834, removed from Steubenville to the city of Cincinnati. Resigning his seat soon afterwards, he resumed the labors of the bar, and ever zealous for the improvement and elevation of the profession, established, in association with others, the Cincinnati law school.

In 1840, upon the dying request of Charles Hammond, the veteran editor of the Cincinnati Gazette, Judge Wright assumed the editorial control of that journal, and retained that position until impaired vision, in 1853, admonished him of the necessity of withdrawing from labors too severe.

Thenceforward engaged in moderate labors, surrounded by affectionate relatives, enjoying the respect and confidence of his fellow-citizens, and manifesting always the liveliest concern in whatever related to the welfare and honor of his State and his country, he lived in tranquil retirement, until called by the Governor of Ohio, with the approbation of the Senate, to take part in the deliberations of this Conference Convention.

It was but a just tribute, sir, to his honored age, illustrated by abilities, by virtues, and by services, that he was unanimously selected as its temporary president. His interest in the great purpose of our assembling was profound and earnest. His labors to promote an auspicious result of its deliberations were active and constant. And when fatal disease assailed his life, and his enfeebled powers yielded to its virulence, his last utterances were of the Constitution and the Union.

Mr. President, Judge Wright was my friend. His approval cheered and encouraged my own humble labors in the service of the State. Pardon me if I mingle private with public grief. He has gone from his last great labor. He was not permitted to witness, upon earth, the result of the mission upon which he and his associates, who here mourn his loss, were sent. God grant, sir, that it may fulfill his wish! God grant that the clouds which now darken over us may speedily disperse, and that through generous counsels and patriotic labors, guided by that good Providence which directed our fathers in its original formation, the Union of our States may be more than ever firmly cemented and established.

Mr. President, I offer the following resolutions :

Resolved, That in the death of our late venerable colleague, the Hon. John C. Wright, we mourn the loss, to the State of Ohio, and to the nation at large, of one of our most sagacious statesmen and distinguished patriots; and to the cause of Union and conciliation, one of its most illustrious supporters.

Resolved, That while we deplore with saddened hearts the affliction with which an Allwise Providence has visited us, we know that no transition from life to immortality could have been more grateful to him who has fallen than this, in which his life has been offered a willing sacrifice in an effort to restore harmony to his distracted country.

Resolved, That the members of this Convention tender their heartfelt sympathies to the family of the deceased in this their great affliction.

Resolved, That these resolutions be spread upon the records of this body, and a copy of the same be transmitted to the family of the deceased.

The Hon. Charles A. Wickliffe, of Kentucky, moved the adoption of the resolutions, and said :

Mr. President, I rise to tender my most cordial sanction and second to the resolutions which have just been read.

Mr. Wright and myself entered the councils of this nation thirty-seven years ago. We served together during a period when party excitement ran high upon questions more of a personal than a constitutional character. I can bear witness not only to his ability, but to his personal integrity, and his purity of political action through our term of service in the House of Representatives. I have seldom met him since we separated at the termination of his service and mine in that body, which occurred at pretty near the same period; but whenever I have met him, I have found him the same stern advocate of the Union, and of constitutional liberty. I rejoiced, therefore, when I found him in this hall on the day we first assembled here. I knew his conservative disposition and principles, and I promised myself that with his aid I could be more useful to my country and to my State than without him. In conversing with him upon the difficulties which now divide and distract our common country, I found him ready and willing, conscientiously and patriotically, to do that which I thought that portion of the country which I represent has a right to demand and expect of those who represent a different portion of our Union. And if my friend from Ohio, (Mr. Chase,) and his colleagues will permit me to mingle my sorrow at the public loss, I will say nothing of the private bereavement of the family of our deceased colleague. I leave him to his country, and to you, with this testimony which I leave to his memory—his honesty of purpose and his patriotic love of country

The Hon. A. W. Loomis, of Pennsylvania, said :

Mr. President, I desire to mingle my sincere regrets with those of the members of this assemblage at the sad and unexpected occurrence which deprived us of an able, experienced, and patriotic associate. My relations with the deceased were, for many years, probably more intimate than those which existed between him and any other member of this Convention. Forty years have elapsed since I first made his acquaintance. He was then in full, active, and extensive practice; a learned lawyer, an accomplished, skillful, and successful advocate. During the succeeding year I came to the bar, and resided and practiced in the same judicial circuit with our departed friend. For many years the most kind and intimate relations existed between us, sometimes colleagues, but usually opponents. So kind and genial was his nature, so fair and liberal his practice, that during our entire intercourse not an unkind word was uttered, and, so far as I know or believe, not an unpleasant feeling existed in the bosom of either.

Though not gifted with the highest order of eloquence, he was clear, distinct, and persuasive. His style of speaking resembled not the babbling brook or the dashing cataract, but usually the limpid stream, gliding gracefully amid fields and fruits and flowers, though sometimes assuming the power and proportions of the majestic river, cutting its sure and certain way to the mighty ocean.

His professional position, his kindness of heart, and genial humor, made him an object of high respect and warm regard among his professional brethren. And now, sir, as memory passes in review the happy hours and pleasant incidents which marked our social and professional intercourse, the smitten heart shrinks in sadness and sorrow from the contemplation of our bereavement. He adorned, sir, the bar, the bench, and the halls of legislation. He discharged, in all the relations of life, his obligations with fidelity. Of him it might be truly said :

> His life hath flowed a sacred stream, in whose calm depth
> The beautiful and pure alone are mirrored;
> Which, though shapes of ill may hover o'er the surface,
> Glides in light, and takes no shadows from them.

But, sir, the great crowning virtue and glory of his life was his acceptance of the mission which brought him here. Though whitened by the frosts of nearly eighty winters, neither lofty mountains nor intervening space could restrain his patriotic heart from a prompt response to the call of his country to mingle his influence in a sincere and sacred effort to save the Constitution and perpetuate the Union. He accepted the great trust; he mingled in our deliberations, and has fallen in the discharge of his duty. He has justly earned a title to the gratitude and respect of his country. May we not, sir, fondly hope that he, who was called from the discharge of such duties to the presence of his God, has passed from the sorrows of earth to the happiness of Heaven, and to the full fruition of joys pure, perfect, and *eternal ?*

The Hon. Thomas L. Ewing, of Ohio, said :

I rise to bear my tribute of respect to the memory of the deceased. I have known him long. On my first entrance into active life, the bar, I found him an able and distinguished member Since that time down to the present day, he has been largely associated, in mind and person, with all the acts and progress, professional and political, of my life. I feel his loss intensely; and I feel it with more regret, because I know that on this occasion his voice would have been potential in our counsels, and would have been united with all of us, who labor most earnestly for the preservation of the Union.

I tender my sympathies to the family of the deceased. I unite with them in their regrets, and in their hopes of the happy future to which he may have attained.

The Hon. William C. Rives, of Virginia, said :

Though wholly unprepared to say anything worthy of the solemnity of this occasion, I feel that I should be wanting, sir, in that sentiment of respect which is due to the character of a distinguished citizen, if I were not to add to what has been so eloquently spoken by others a few words of personal recollection in regard to our deceased friend, Judge Wright. It so happened that we entered the public councils of the country at the same moment, and continued in them for the same period of time. It is now just thirty-seven years since I had the pleasure of meeting Judge Wright, for the first time, in the House of Representatives of the United States. I may be permitted to say, that there were giants in those days. My honorable friend from Kentucky, (Governor Wickliffe,) who has already so feelingly addressed the Convention, will recollect that on the roll of the House of Representatives at that time stood the names of Webster and Everett, of Oakley and of Storrs, of Sergeant and of Hemphill, of Lewis McLane, of the immortal Clay, and Barbour, and Randall, and other gentlemen known to fame, from the State which I have the honor to represent in this body, and Livingston, of Louisiana, McDuffie, and Hamilton, of South Carolina, and other gentlemen who, on the spur of the occasion, I am not now able to recall, but whose names will forever shine upon the rolls of their country's glory. And yet in that body Judge Wright, then in the maturity of his powers, though not previously known to the nation, vindicated an equal rank in debate with those gentlemen whose names I have mentioned. Sir, I shall never forget with what earnestness, with what manliness, with what integrity, with what ability, he ever uttered his convictions of public duty, whatever they were, in that consecrated hall.

After remaining there, I think, for six years, he retired to his own State for the purpose of assuming the duties of a highly important and dignified office, which was soon followed by his retirement into the bosom of private life, where he met a rich and ample solace for the storms of his public career. He was followed there by the respect of his fellow-citizens throughout the country; and the confidence of his own State, as we have recently seen, by his being called from that honorable retirement to take part in the grave and solemn duties of this assembly. Sir, he came among us in obedience to the solemn call of patriotic duty, at a most exigent and distressing period in our national annals. He came here on an errand of peace, in the spirit of peace and conciliation. Such was the feeling entertained towards him by the whole of this assembly, that without the slightest preconcert, so far as I know, he was invited by general consent to preside during the preliminary stages of the organization of this Convention. I had the opportunity, from time to time, of private conversation with the aged statesman. I found no member of the assembly I met here—and, indeed, I have found nowhere any citizen of this wide Republic of ours—whose heart was more deeply imbued with the spirit of conciliation and of peace, of that spirit which was so solemnly and impressively uttered in his last prayer, "May the Union be preserved." Sir, it is not given to mortal man to choose the manner of his death; but if such were the privilege accorded to any human being, what more glorious end could he, appreciating a true fame, covet than that which has been the lot of our departed friend ! Sir, I speak what I feel, and I dare say I express a sentiment which has impressed itself upon many other bosoms in this

5

assembly, when I say that his sudden death in the midst of our deliberations, seems to me to exalt—in some degree, to canonize—our labors. This visible manifestation of the hand of God among us brings us in the immediate presence of those solemn responsibilities which attach themselves to the discharge of our duties here. I doubt not that every member of this assembly is already deeply impressed with the solemnity of those duties, and I feel convinced that there are few, if any, in this assembly, who would not lay down their fleeting and feverish existence, and follow our deceased brother to his final account, if by doing so they could restore peace and harmony to this glorious Republic of ours.

It does not become me to make any professions of devotion to my country—to my whole country ! But this I will say, in the spirit of the last prayer of my friend, that I should regard my poor life, such as it is, a cheap purchase—the cheapest imaginable purchase—for that great boon to our country, the restoration of its peace, of its harmony, of its unity, of its ancient confederated strength and glory.

The question was taken, and the resolutions were unanimously adopted. The body of Mr. Wright was then brought into the hall, preceded by the Rev. Dr. Hall, who read the impressive funeral service of the Episcopal Church. A number of the members of the family, and of the friends of the deceased, were present during the services. The funeral cortege proceeded from the hall to the depot of the Baltimore and Ohio railroad.*

The following gentlemen acted as pall-bearers on the occasion:

Mr. EWING,	Mr. CHASE,
Mr. HITCHCOCK,	Mr. LOOMIS,
Mr. BACKUS,	Mr. GROESBECK,
Mr. WOLCOTT,	Mr. STANTON,
Mr. SHERMAN,	Mr. HARLAN,
Mr. VINTON,	Mr. GURLEY.

By resolution of the Committee, the proceedings were reported in full, and ordered to be printed.

---

*FUNERAL SERVICES OF HON. JOHN C. WRIGHT.

CINCINNATI, *February* 17, 1861.

The funeral of the late Judge Wright was very largely attended yesterday afternoon, from his residence on west Sixth street. The funeral service of the Episcopal Church was read by Rev. Dr. Greenleaf, Rector of St. Paul's, of which the deceased was a member. The remains were inclosed in a double mahogany coffin, on the lid of which was a silver plate with the inscription :

"JOHN C. WRIGHT,
BORN Aug. 10, 1784,
DIED Feb. 13, 1861."

In consequence of the large attendance the coffin was placed on the pavement in front of the residence, and the members of the bar, railroad men, and citizens, formed in procession, passed by and took a last look at the face with which they had been so long familiar. The coffin, covered with a black velvet pall, was placed in a hearse and conveyed to the depot of the Cincinnati, Hamilton, and Dayton Railroad, followed by carriages with relations and friends. The pall-bearers were :

NICHOLAS LONGWORTH, Esq.,	JUDGE ESTE,
JUDGE LEVITT,	JUDGE STORER,
CHARLES STETSON, Esq.,	CHARLES FOX, Esq.,
ADAM RIDDLE, Esq.,	E. S. HAINES, Esq.,
V. WORTHINGTON, Esq.,	GEORGE CARLISLE, Esq.,

JOHN P. FOOTE, Esq.

Arrived at the depot, the remains were placed in the front car of a special train of nine cars, in charge of Mr. Potter, conductor. The train moved to the sacred resting place of the dead, slowly, as became the solemnity of the occasion. Another hearse and carriages had been provided at the grounds, and the procession wound its way through the avenues towards the vault, where the services were concluded, and with the words, "earth to earth, dust to dust," were committed to the tomb all that was earthly of him who was so honored in life and lamented in death.

FURTHER OF THE ILLNESS AND DEATH OF JUDGE WRIGHT.

Dr. Miller, of Washington, the physician in attendance upon Hon. John C. Wright during his last illness in that place, states that Mr. Wright had been laboring under chronic bronchitis for many years ; that he had taken cold, which terminated in effusion in the lungs, and that he was unable to throw off the fluid which accumulated, on account of paralysis of the lungs. The result was suffocation.

Judge Wright was entirely conscious to within a few hours of his death. At ten o'clock Wednesday morning last, he received a letter from his wife, and, it having been read to him, he struggled to sit up to reply to it, but found himself unable to do so. At eleven o'clock, seeming revived, he called upon his son to bring and read to him the Federal Constitution, and repeated that part pertaining to the counting of the votes for President and Vice President, in the performance of the duty under which he supposed the two houses of Congress to be then engaged. At twelve o'clock he urged his son, with other friends, to leave him for the Convention, and at the same time exacted a promise from his son, that, if he should be compelled to attend his body home, he would at once return and resume his duties as Secretary of the Convention.—*Cincinnati Gazette.*

WASHINGTON CITY, *February* 15, 1861.

The Convention met pursuant to adjournment.

President Tyler in the chair.

The Convention was opened with prayer by Rev. Mr. Renner.

The journals of the 13th and the special session of the 14th were read and approved.

The President laid before the Convention a communication from Horatio Stone, extending an invitation to members of the Convention to visit his *studio;* which was read, and laid on the table.

The President presented to the Convention a resolution of the House of Representatives, tendering admission to the floor of the House to members of the Convention; in accordance with which cards of admission had been sent.

The President also presented a letter from J. E. Sands, proffering to the Convention some flags with historical reminiscences, to be placed in this hall during its session; which was read, and laid on the table.

Also a communication from Horatio G. Warner, which was received, and laid on the table.

Mr. Summers, from the Committee on Credentials, presented a telegraph dispatch from the Governor of Ohio, appointing C. P. Wolcott a commissioner in the place of John C. Wright, deceased.

Mr. Wolcott's name was entered on the list of members.

Mr. Orth, of Indiana, offered the following resolutions:

Resolved, That rules sixteen (16) and eighteen (18) of this Convention be, and the same are hereby, rescinded.

Resolved, That the President is hereby authorized to grant cards of admission to reporters of the press not exceeding —— in number, which shall entitle them to seats on the floor of the Convention, for the purpose of reporting its proceedings.

Resolved, That no person be admitted to the floor of this Convention, except the members, officers, or reporters.

After discussion by Messrs. Wickliffe and Orth, on motion of Mr. Randolph, the resolutions were laid on the table.

Mr. Guthrie, from the Committee of one from each State, made a report, and submitted the following proposed amendments of the Constitution:

ARTICLE 1. In all the territory of the United States, not embraced within the limits of the Cherokee treaty grant, north of a line from east to west, on the parallel of 36 degrees 30 minutes, north latitude, involuntary servitude, except in punishment of crime, is prohibited whilst it shall be under a Territorial government; and in all the territory south of said line, the status of persons owing service or labor as it now exists shall not be changed by law while such territory shall be under a Territorial government; and neither Congress nor the Territorial government shall have power to hinder or prevent the taking to said territory of persons held to labor or involuntary service, within the United States, according to the laws or usages of the State from which such persons may be taken, nor to impair the rights arising out of said relations, which shall be subject to judicial cognizance in the federal courts, according to the common law; and when any territory north or south of said line, within such boundary as Congress may prescribe, shall contain a population required for a member of Congress, according to the then federal ratio of representation, it shall, if its form of government be republican, be admitted into the Union on an equal footing with the original States, with or without involuntary service or labor, as the constitution of such new State may provide.

ARTICLE 2. Territory shall not be acquired by the United States, unless by treaty; nor, except for naval and commercial stations and depots, unless such treaty shall be ratified by four fifths of all members of the Senate.

ARTICLE 3. Neither the Constitution, nor any amendment thereof, shall be construed to give Congress power to regulate, abolish, or control, within any State or Territory of the United States, the relation established or recognized by the laws thereof touching persons bound to labor or involuntary service therein, nor to interfere with or abolish involuntary service in the District of Columbia without the consent of Maryland and without the consent of the owners, or making the owners who do not consent just compensation; nor the power to interfere with or prohibit Representatives and others from bringing with them to the city of Washington, retaining, and taking away, persons so bound to labor; nor the power to interfere with or abolish involuntary service in places under the exclusive jurisdiction of the United States within those States and Territories where the same is established or recognized; nor the power to prohibit the removal or transportation, by land, sea, or river, of persons held to labor or involuntary service in any State or Territory of the United States to any other State or Territory thereof where it is established or recognized by law or usage; and the right during transportation of touching at ports, shores, and landings, and of landing in case of distress, shall exist. Nor shall Congress have power to authorize any higher rate of taxation on persons bound to labor than on land.

ARTICLE 4. The third paragraph of the second section of the fourth article of the Constitution shall not be construed to prevent any of the States, by appropriate legislation, and through the action of their judicial and ministerial officers, from enforcing the delivery of fugitives from labor to the person to whom such service or labor is due.

ARTICLE 5. The foreign slave trade and the importation of slaves into the United States and their Territories, from places beyond the present limits thereof, are forever prohibited.

ARTICLE 6. The first, second, third, and fifth articles, together with this article, of these amendments, and the third paragraph of the second section of the first article of the Constitution, and the third paragraph of the second section of the fourth article thereof, shall not be amended or abolished without the consent of all the States.

ARTICLE 7. Congress shall provide by law that the United States shall pay to the owner the full value of his fugitive from labor, in all cases where the marshal or other officer, whose duty it was to arrest such fugitive, was prevented from so doing by violence or intimidation, or when, after arrest, such fugitive was rescued by force, and the owner thereby prevented and obstructed in the pursuit of his remedy for the recovery of such fugitive.

Mr. Baldwin, from the same committee, submitted the following report:

The undersigned, comprising a part of the minority of the committee of one from each State, to whom was referred the consideration of the resolutions of the State of Virginia and the other States represented, and all propositions for the adjustment of existing differences between the States, with authority to report what they deem right, necessary, and proper to restore harmony and preserve the Union, and report thereon, entered upon the duties of the committee with an anxious desire that they might be able to unite in the recommendation of some plan which, on due deliberation, should seem best adapted to maintain the dignity and authority of the Government of the United States, and, at the same time, secure to the people of every section that perfect equality of right to which they are entitled.

Convened, as we are, on the invitation of the Governor of Virginia, in pursuance of the resolutions of the General Assembly of that State, with an accompanying expression of the deliberate opinion of that body that, unless the unhappy controversy which now divides the States shall be satisfactorily adjusted, a permanent dissolution of the Union is inevitable; and, being earnestly desirous of an adjustment thereof, in concurrence with Virginia, in the spirit in which the Constitution was originally formed, and consistently with its principles, so as to afford to the people of all the States adequate security for all their rights, the attention of the undersigned was necessarily led to the consideration of the extent and equality of our powers, and to the propriety and expediency, under existing circumstances, of a recommendation by this Conference Convention of any specific action by Congress, whether of ordinary legislation, or in reference to constitutional amendments to be proposed by Congress on its own responsibility to the States.

A portion of the members of this Convention are delegated by the Legislatures of their respective States, and are required to act under their supervision and control, while others are the representatives only of the Executives of their States, and, having no opportunity of consulting the immediate representatives of the people, can only act on their individual responsibility.

Among the resolutions and propositions suggesting modes of adjustment appropriate to this occasion which were brought to the notice of the committee, were the resolutions of the State of Kentucky recommending to her sister States to unite with her in an application to Congress for the calling of a convention in the mode prescribed by the Constitution for proposing amendments thereto.

The undersigned, for the reasons set forth in the accompanying resolution, and others which have been herein indicated, is of opinion that the mode of adjustment by a general convention, as proposed by Kentucky, is the one which affords the best assurance of an adjustment acceptable to the people of every section, as it will afford to all the States who may desire amendments an opportunity of preparing them with care and deliberation, and in such form as they may deem it expedient to prescribe, to be submitted to the consideration and deliberate action of delegates duly chosen and invested with equal powers from all the States.

The undersigned did not, therefore, deem it expedient that any of the measures of adjustment proposed by the majority of the committee should be reported to this body to be discussed or acted upon by them, and he respectfully submits, as a substitute for the articles of amendment to the Constitution, reported by the majority of the committee, the following preamble and resolution, and respectfully recommends the adoption thereof.

ROGER S. BALDWIN.

Whereas, Unhappy differences exist which have alienated from each other portions of the people of the United States to such an extent as seriously to disturb the peace of the nation, and impair the regular and efficient action of the Government within the sphere of its constitutional powers and duties:

And whereas, the Legislature of the State of Kentucky has made application to Congress to call a convention for proposing amendments to the Constitution of the United States:

And whereas, it is believed to be the opinion of the people of other States that amendments to the Constitution are or may become necessary to secure to the people of the United States, of every section, the full and equal enjoyment of their rights and liberties, so far as the same may depend for their security and protection on the powers granted to or withheld from the General Government, in pursuance of the national purposes for which it was ordained and established:

And whereas, it may be expedient that such amendments as any of the States may desire to have proposed, should be presented to the convention in such form as the respective States desiring the same may deem proper:

This convention does, therefore, recommend to the several States to unite with Kentucky in her application to Congress to call a convention for proposing amendments to the Constitution of the United States, to be submitted to the Legislatures of the several States, or to conventions therein, for ratification, as the one or the other mode of ratification may be proposed by Congress, in accordance with the provision in the fifth article of the Constitution.

Mr. Field, of New York, and Mr. Crowninshield, of Massachusetts, of the same committee, stated that they had not concurred in the majority report.

Mr. Seddon, of Virginia, from the same committee, submitted the following report:

The undersigned, acting on the recommendation of the commissioners from the State of Virginia, as a member of the committee appointed by this Convention to consider and recommend propositions of adjustment, has not been so happy as to accord with the report submitted by the majority ; and as he more widely dissents from the opinions entertained by the other dissenting members, he feels constrained, in vindication of his position and opinions, to present on his part this brief report, recommending, as a substitute for the report of the majority, a proposition subjoined. To this course he feels the more impelled, by deference to the resolutions of the General Assembly of his State, inviting the assemblage of this Convention, and suggesting a basis of adjustment. These resolutions declare, that, " in the opinion of the General Assembly of Virginia, the propositions embraced in the resolutions presented to the Senate of the United States by the Hon. John J. Crittenden, so modified as that the first article proposed as an amendment to the Constitution of the United States, shall apply to all the territory of the United States now held, or hereafter acquired, south of latitude 36 degrees 30 minutes, and provided that slavery of the African race shall be effectually protected as property therein during the continuance of the Territorial government, and the fourth article shall secure to the owners of slaves the right of transit with their slaves between and through the non-slaveholding States or Territories, constitute the basis of such an adjustment of the unhappy controversy which now divides the States of this confederacy, as would be accepted by the people of this Commonwealth."

From this resolution, it is clear that the General Assembly, in its declared opinion of what would be acceptable to the people of Virginia, not only required the Crittenden propositions as a basis, but also held the modifications suggested in addition essential. In this the undersigned fully concurs. But, in his opinion, the propositions reported by the majority do not give, but materially weaken, the Crittenden propositions themselves, and fail to accord the modifications suggested. The undersigned, therefore, feels it his duty to submit and recommend, as a substitute, the resolutions referred to, as proposed by the Hon. John J. Crittenden, with the incorporation of the modifications suggested by Virginia explicitly expressed, and with some alterations on points which, he is assured, would make them more acceptable to that State, and, as he hopes, to the whole Union. The propositions submitted are appended, marked No. 1

The undersigned, while contenting himself in the spirit of the action taken by the General Assembly of his State, with the proposal of that substitute for the majority report, would be untrue to his own convictions, shared, as he believes, by the majority of the Commissioners from Virginia, and to his sense of duty, if he did not emphatically declare, as his settled and deliberate judgment, that for permanent safety in this Union to the slaveholding States, and the restoration of integrity to the Union, and harmony and peace to the country, a guarantee of actual power in the Constitution and in the working of the Government to the slaveholding and minority section, is indispensable. How such guarantee might be most wisely contrived and judiciously adjusted to the frame of the Government, the undersigned forbears now to inquire. He is not exclusively addicted to any special plan, but believing that such guarantee might be adequately afforded by a partition of power in the Senate between the two sections, and by a recognition that ours is a Union of freedom and consent, not constraint and force, he respectfully, submits, for consideration by members of the Convention, the plan hereto appended, marked No. 2.

Whether he shall feel bound to invoke the action of the Convention upon it, may depend on the future manifestations of sentiment in this body.

All which is respectfully submitted.

JAMES A. SEDDON,
Commissioner from Va.

FEBRUARY 15, 1861.

———

No. 1.

JOINT RESOLUTIONS proposing certain amendments to the Constitution of the United States.

WHEREAS, Serious and alarming dissensions have arisen between the Northern and Southern States, concerning the rights and security of the rights of the slaveholding States, and especially their rights in the common territory of the United States ; and whereas, it is eminently desirable and proper that those dissensions, which now threaten the very existence of this Union, should be permanently quieted and settled by constitutional provisions, which shall do equal justice to all sections, and thereby restore to the people that peace and good will which ought to prevail between all the citizens of the United States : therefore,

Resolved, by this Convention, that the following articles are hereby approved and submitted to the Congress of the United States, with the request that they may, by the requisite constitutional majority of two thirds, be recommended to the respective States of the Union, to be, when ratified by conventions of three fourths of the States, valid and operative as amendments of the Constitution of the Union.

ARTICLE 1. In all the territory of the United States now held, or hereafter acquired, situate north of latitude thirty-six degrees and thirty minutes, slavery or involuntary servitude, except as a punishment for crime, is prohibited, while such territory shall remain under territorial government. In all the territory south of said line of latitude slavery of the African race is hereby recognized as existing, and shall not be interfered with by Congress ; but hall be protected as property by all the departments of the territorial government during its continuance ; and when any territory north or south of said line, within such boundaries as Congress may prescribe, shall contain the population requisite for a member of Congress, according to the then federal ratio of representation of the people of the United States, it shall, if its form of government be republican, be admitted into the Union on an equal footing with the original States, with or without slavery, as the constitution of such new State may provide.

ARTICLE 2. Congress shall have no power to abolish slavery in places under its exclusive jurisdiction, and situate within the limits of States that permit the holding of slaves.

ARTICLE 3. Congress shall have no power to abolish slavery within the District of Columbia, so long as it exists in the adjoining States of Virginia and Maryland, or either, nor without the consent of the free white inhabitants, nor without just compensation first made to such owners of slaves as do not consent to such abolishment. Nor shall Congress at any time prohibit officers of the Federal Government, or members of Congress, whose duties require them to be in said District, from bringing with them their slaves, and holding them as such during the time their duties may require them to remain there, and afterwards taking them from the District.

ARTICLE 4. Congress shall have no power to prohibit or hinder the transportation of slaves from one State to another, or to a Territory in which slaves are by law permitted to be held, whether that transportation be by land, navigable rivers, or by the sea. And if such transportation be by sea, the slaves shall be protected as property by the Federal Government. And the right of transit by the owners with their slaves, in passing to or from one slaveholding State or Territory to another, between and through the non-slaveholding States and Territories, shall be protected. And in imposing direct taxes pursuant to the Constitution, Congress shall have no power to impose on slaves a higher rate of tax than on land, according to their just value.

ARTICLE 5. That, in addition to the provisions of the third paragraph of the second section of the fourth article of the Constitution of the United States, Congress shall provide by law, that the United States shall pay to the owner who shall apply for it, the full value of his fugitive slave, in all cases, when the marshal, or other officer, whose duty it was to arrest said fugitive, was prevented from so doing by violence or intimidation, or when, after arrest, said fugitive was rescued by force, and the owner thereby prevented and obstructed in the pursuit of his remedy for the recovery of his fugitive slave, under the said clause of the Constitution and the laws made in pursuance thereof. And in all such cases, when the United States shall pay for such fugitive, they shall reimburse themselves by imposing and collecting a tax on the county or city in which said violence, intimidation, or rescue was committed, equal in amount to the sum paid by them, with the addition of interest and the costs of collection; and the said county or city, after it has paid said amount to the United States, may, for its indemnity, sue and recover from the wrong-doers, or rescuers, by whom the owner was prevented from the recovery of his fugitive slave, in like manner as the owner himself might have sued and recovered

ARTICLE 6. No future amendment of the Constitution shall affect the five preceding articles, nor the third paragraph of the second section of the first article of the Constitution, nor the third paragraph of the second section of the fourth article of said Constitution, and no amendment shall be made to the Constitution which will authorize or give to Congress any power to abolish or interfere with slavery in any of the States by whose laws it is or may be allowed or permitted.

. ARTICLE 7. SEC. 1. The elective franchise and the right to hold office, whether federal, State, territorial, or municipal, shall not be exercised by persons who are, in whole or in part, of the African race.

And whereas, also, besides those causes of dissension embraced in the foregoing amendments proposed to the Constitution of the United States, there are others which come within the jurisdiction of Congress, and may be remedied by its legislative power; and whereas, it is the desire of this Convention, as far as its influence may extend, to remove all just cause for the popular discontent and agitation which now disturb the peace of the country, and threaten the stability of its institutions: therefore,

1. *Resolved*, That the laws now in force for the recovery of fugitive slaves are in strict pursuance of the plain and mandatory provisions of the Constitution, and have been sanctioned as valid and constitutional by the judgment of the Supreme Court of the United States; that the slaveholding States are entitled to the faithful observance and execution of those laws, and that they ought not to be repealed or so modified or changed as to impair their efficiency; and that laws ought to be made for the punishment of those who attempt, by rescue of the slave or other illegal means, to hinder or defeat the due execution of said laws.

2. That all State laws which conflict with the fugitive slave acts, or any other constitutional acts of Congress, or which in their operation impede, hinder, or delay the free course and due execution of any of said acts, are null and void by the plain provisions of the Constitution of the United States. Yet those State laws, void as they are, have given color to practices, and led to consequences which have obstructed the due administration and execution of acts of Congress, and especially the acts for the delivery of fugitive slaves, and have thereby contributed much to the discord and commotion now prevailing. This Convention, therefore, in the present perilous juncture, does not deem it improper, respectfully and earnestly, to recommend the repeal of those laws to the several States which have enacted them, or such legislative corrections or explanations of them as may prevent their being used or perverted to such mischievous purposes.

3. That the act of the eighteenth of September, eighteen hundred and fifty, commonly called the fugitive slave law, ought to be so amended as to make the fee of the commissioner, mentioned in the eighth section of the act, equal in amount, in the cases decided by him, whether his decision be in favor of or against the claimant. And to avoid misconstruction, the last clause of the fifth section of said act, which authorizes the person holding a warrant for the arrest or detention of a fugitive slave to summon to his aid the posse comitatus, and which declares it to be the duty of all good citizens to assist him in its execution, ought to be so amended as to expressly limit the authority and duty to cases in which there shall be resistance, or danger of resistance or rescue.

4. That the laws for the suppression of the African slave trade, and especially those prohibiting the importation of slaves into the United States, ought to be made effectual, and ought to be thoroughly executed, and all further enactments necessary to those ends ought to be promptly made.

No. 2.

PROPOSED AMENDMENTS BY MR. SEDDON.

To secure concert and promote harmony between the slaveholding and non-slaveholding sections of the Union, the assent of the majority of the Senators from the slaveholding States, and of the majority of the Senators from the non-slaveholding States, shall be requisite to the validity of all action of the Senate, on which the ayes and noes may be called by five Senators.

And on a written declaration, signed and presented for record on the journal of the Senate by a majority of the Senators from either the non-slaveholding or slaveholding States, of their want of confidence in any officer or appointee of the Executive, exercising functions exclusively or continuously within the class of States, or any of them, which the signers represent, then such officer shall be removed by the Executive; and if not removed at the expiration of ten days from the presentation of such declaration, the office shall be deemed vacant, and open to new appointment.

The connection of every State with the Union is recognized as depending on the continuing assent of its people, and compulsion shall in no case, nor under any form, be attempted by the government of the Union against a State acting in its collective or organic capacity. Any State, by the action of a convention of its people, assembled pursuant to a law of its Legislature, is held entitled to dissolve its relation to the Federal Government, and withdraw from the Union; and, on due notice given of such withdrawal to the Executive of the Union, he shall appoint two commissioners, to meet two commissioners to be appointed by the Governor of the State, who, with the aid, if needed from the disagreement of the commissioners, of an umpire, to be selected by a majority of them, shall equitably adjudicate and determine finally a partition of the rights and obligations of the withdrawing State; and such adjudication and partition being accomplished, the withdrawal of such State shall be recognized by the Executive, and announced by public proclamation to the world.

But such withdrawing State shall not afterwards be re-admitted into the Union without the assent of two thirds of the States constituting the Union at the time of the proposed re-admission.

Mr. Coalter, of Missouri, stated the basis of the action of that State.

Mr. Wickliffe, of Kentucky, moved the printing of the reports, and that they be made the order of the day for to-morrow, at 12 o'clock; which, after discussion, was adopted.

Mr. Chase, of Ohio, moved the printing of all resolutions of the several States in relation to the subjects before this Convention; which was ordered.

Mr. Wickliffe offered the following preamble and resolutions:

The second section of the 4th article of the Constitution of the United States declares, "that no person held to service or labor in one State, under the laws thereof, escaping into another, shall, in consequence of any law or regulation therein, be discharged from such service or labor, but shall be delivered up on claim of the party to whom such service or labor may be due."

This clause is one of the compromises without which no Constitution would have been adopted. It was a guarantee to the States, in which such labor and service existed by law, that their rights should be respected and regarded by all the States; and it is not within the competency of any State to disregard the obligations it imposes, or to render it valueless by legislative enactments. And whereas, the House of Representatives of the United States did, on the —— of February, by unanimous vote, declare that neither the Congress of the United States, nor the people or government of any non-slaveholding State, has the constitutional right to legislate upon, or to interfere with, slavery in any slaveholding State in the Union.

This declaration is regarded by this Convention as an admission that the statutes of those States, passed for the purpose of defeating the provision of the Constitution aforesaid, and the laws of Congress made to enforce the just and proper execution of this constitutional guarantee, are in violation of the supreme law of the land.

The provisions of the statutes in many of the non-slaveholding States, commonly known and called "personal liberty bills," amount in their consequences to a practical nullification of the acts of Congress of February 12th, 1793, and September 18th, 1850, and are in violation of the 2d section of the 4th article of the Constitution, as before stated. That the spirit of those statutes appears to be repugnant to the principles of compromise and mutual and liberal concessions which dictated the section of the Constitution in question, and which pervades every part of that instrument. It is, therefore, respectfully requested by this Convention that the several States abrogate all such obnoxious enactments.

That the spirit of comity between the States, and the spirit of unity and fraternity which should actuate all the people of these United States, require that complete right and security of transit with all persons who owe them service or labor should be allowed to the citizens of each State by the laws of every other State.

Resolved, That a copy of the foregoing be sent by the President of this Convention to the Governors of each of the free States, as the deliberate judgment and opinion of this Convention, and that he request the same be laid before their respective Legislatures.

The Convention then adjourned until 12 o'clock, to-morrow.

———

WASHINGTON CITY, February 16, 1861.

The Convention met pursuant to adjournment.

President Tyler in the chair.

Prayer was offered by Rev. Dr. Sunderland.

The journal of the preceding day was read and approved.

The President laid before the Convention a communication from W. C. Jewett, which was received and laid on the table.

Mr. Wickliffe offered the following resolution:

Resolved, That in the discussions which may take place in this Convention upon any questions, no member shall be allowed to speak longer than thirty minutes.

Which, after debate thereon, was postponed by the mover until Tuesday.

Mr. Crisfield moved the hour of meeting of the Convention be at ten o'clock, which was amended to eleven o'clock, A. M., and adopted.

Mr. Chase moved to amend the first rule by inserting after the word "represented," the following: "The yeas and nays of the delegates from each State, on any question, shall be entered on the Journal when it is desired by any delegate." Which was not agreed to.

Mr. Wickliffe, from the Committee on Organization, offered the following resolution, which was adopted.

Resolved, That the 11th Rule of this Convention be so amended as to allow an appeal from the decision of the President, which appeal shall be decided without debate.

Mr. Johnson, of Maryland, gave notice that he should move to insert the word *present* before the word *Territories*, in the first line of the first section of the majority report, so as to conform to the intention of the majority of the committee.

On motion, adjourned.

———

WASHINGTON CITY, *February* 18, 1861.

The convention met pursuant to adjournment.

President Tyler in the chair.

The proceedings were opened with prayer by the Rev. Dr. Gurley.

The journal of Saturday was read and approved.

Mr. Chittenden, of Vermont, offered the following resolution:

Resolved, That the rules of this Convention be so far modified as to require the Secretary to employ a competent stenographer, who shall write down and preserve accurate notes of the debates and other proceedings of this body, which notes shall not be communicated to any person, nor shall copies thereof be taken, nor shall the same be made public until after the final adjournment of this Convention, except in pursuance of a vote authorizing their publication.

Mr. Pollock, of Pennsylvania, moved to lay the resolution upon the table.

A vote by States was taken.

AYES—Connecticut, Rhode Island, New Jersey, Delaware, Maryland, Kentucky, Tennessee, North Carolina, Missouri, Virginia, and Pennsylvania—11.

NOES—Maine, Vermont, New Hampshire, Massachusetts, Indiana, Illinois, Iowa, and New York—8.

Ohio, being divided, did not vote.

The motion to lay upon the table was thereupon declared carried.

Mr. Tuck, of New Hampshire, presented the following address and resolutions; which were read, and on motion, ordered to be laid on the table and printed:

To THE PEOPLE OF THE UNITED STATES :

This Convention of Conference, composed in part of commissioners appointed in accordance with the legislative action of sundry States, and in part of commissioners appointed by the Governors of sundry other States, in compliance with an invitation by the General Assembly of Virginia, met in Washington on the 4th February, 1861. Although constituting a body unknown to the Constitution and laws, yet being delegated for the purpose, and having carefully considered the existing dangers and dissensions, and having brought their proceedings to a close, publish this address, and the accompanying resolutions, as the result of their deliberations.

We recognize and deplore the divisions and distractions which now afflict our country, interrupt its prosperity, disturb its peace, and endanger the Union of the States ; but we repel the conclusion that any alienations or dissensions exist which are irreconcilable, which justify attempts at revolution, or which the patriotism and fraternal sentiments of the people, and the interests and honor of the whole nation, will not overcome.

6

In a country embracing the central and most important portion of a continent, among a people now numbering over thirty millions, diversities of opinion inevitably exist; and rivalries, intensified at times by local interests and sectional attachments, must often occur; yet we do not doubt that the theory of our government is the best which is possible for this nation, that the Union of the States is of vital importance, and that the Constitution, which expresses the combined wisdom of the illustrious founders of the government, is still the palladium of our liberties, adequate to every emergency, and justly entitled to the support of every good citizen.

It embraces, in its provisions and spirit, all the defense and protection which any section of the country can rightfully demand, or honorably concede.

Adopted with primary reference to the wants of five millions of people, but with the wisest reference to future expansion and development, it has carried us onward with a rapid increase of numbers, an accumulation of wealth, and a degree of happiness and general prosperity never attained by any nation.

Whatever branch of industry, or whatever staple production shall become, in the possible changes of the future, the leading interest of the country, thereby creating unforeseen complications or new conflicts of opinion and interest, the Constitution of the United States, properly understood, and fairly enforced, is equal to every exigency, a shield and defense to all in every time of need. If, however, by reason of a change in circumstance, or for any cause, a portion of the people believe they ought to have their rights more exactly defined or more fully explained in the Constitution, it is their duty, in accordance with its provisions, to seek a remedy by way of amendment to that instrument; and it is the duty of all the States to concur in such amendments as may be found necessary to insure equal and exact justice to all.

In order, therefore, to announce to the country the sentiments of this Convention, respecting not only the remedy which should be sought for existing discontents, but also to communicate to the public what we believe to be the patriotic sentiment of the country, we adopt the following resolutions:

1st. *Resolved*, That this Convention recognize the well understood proposition that the Constitution of the United States gives no power to Congress, or any branch of the Federal Government to interfere in any manner with slavery in any of the States; and we are assured, by abundant testimony, that neither of the great political organizations existing in the country contemplates a violation of the spirit of the Constitution in this regard, or the procuring of any amendment thereof, by which Congress, or any department of the General Government, shall ever have jurisdiction over slavery in any of the States.

2d. *Resolved*, That the Constitution was ordained and established, as set forth in the preamble, by the people of the United States, in order to form a more perfect Union, establish justice, insure domestic tranquility, provide for the common defense, promote the general welfare, and secure the blessings of liberty to themselves and their posterity; and when the people of any State are not in full enjoyment of all the benefits intended to be secured to them by the Constitution, or their rights under it are disregarded, their tranquility disturbed, their prosperity retarded, or their liberty imperiled by the people of any other State, full and adequate redress can and ought to be provided for such grievances.

3d. *Resolved*, That this Convention recommend to the Legislatures of the several States of the Union to follow the example of the Legislatures of the States of Kentucky and of Illinois, in applying to Congress to call a Convention for the proposing of amendments to the Constitution of the United States, pursuant to the fifth article thereof.

Mr. Guthrie offered the following resolution, which was adopted:

Resolved, That if the President shall choose to speak on any question, he may for the occasion call any member to preside.

Mr. Meredith gave notice of his intent to offer a proposition, as follows; which was read, laid upon the table, and ordered to be printed:

ARTICLE —. That Congress shall divide all the territory of the United States into convenient portions, each containing not less than sixty thousand square miles, and shall establish in each a Territorial Government; the several Territorial Legislatures, whether heretofore constituted or hereafter to be constituted, shall have all the legislative powers now vested in the respective States of this Union; and whenever any Territory, having a population sufficient, according to the ratio existing at the time, to entitle it to one member of Congress, shall form a republican constitution, and apply to Congress for admission as a State, Congress shall admit the same as a State accordingly.

Mr. Wickliffe moved that the journal of the Convention up to the present day be printed.

Mr. Goodrich moved to amend, by inserting "that it be printed from day to day;" which amendment was adopted, and the resolution, as amended, passed.

The order of the day having been called,

Mr. Johnson moved the adoption of the amendments submitted by him on the 16th.

Mr. Reid, of North Carolina, moved to add to the proposed amendment of Mr. Johnson the words "and future;" whereupon a vote was taken by States, with the following result:

Ayes—New Jersey, Delaware, Maryland, Kentucky, Tennessee, North Carolina, Missouri, and Virginia—8.

Noes—Vermont, Maine, New Hampshire, Massachusetts, Connecticut, Rhode Island, Ohio, Indiana, Illinois, Pennsylvania, New York, and Iowa—12.

So the amendment was lost.

A debate ensued on the amendment of Mr. Johnson, which was adopted; the first section of the majority report, as amended, reading as follows:

Sec. 1. In all the *present* territory of the United States, not embraced within the limits of the Cherokee treaty grant, north of a line from east to west, on the parallel of 36 degrees 30 minutes north latitude, involuntary servitude, except in punishment of crime, is prohibited whilst it shall be under a Territorial government; and in all the *present* territory south of said line, &c.

The Convention, on motion, adjourned at 4, P. M.

———

WASHINGTON CITY, *February* 19, 1861.

Convention met at 11, A. M., pursuant to adjournment. President Tyler in the chair.

Proceedings opened by prayer.

The journal of proceedings was read, amended, and approved.

Mr. Summers, from the Committee on Credentials, reported that the Committee had received the credentials of the Hon. Francis Granger, as a Commissioner of the State of New York, in the place of Addison Gardiner; and the list of members was altered accordingly.

Mr. Wickliffe called up the following resolution, heretofore offered by him, and laid upon the table:

Resolved, That in the discussions which may take place in this Convention upon any questions, no member shall be allowed to speak longer than thirty minutes.

Mr. Davis, of North Carolina, moved to amend, by striking out *thirty minutes*, and inserting *ten minutes*.

Mr. Caruthers moved further to amend by adding the following:

"And that all debates shall cease at 3 o'clock to-day, and the vote taken on such amendments as may be offered, and then on the report."

It was moved to lay "the whole subject upon the table." A division was called for, the result of which was as follows:—ayes 49, nays 54.

So the motion to lay on the table was not agreed to.

Mr. Randolph, of New Jersey, offered the following, as a substitute for the resolution and amendments:

Resolved, That this Convention will hold two sessions daily, viz: From 10 o'clock, A. M., to 4 o'clock, P. M.; and from 8 to 10 o'clock, P. M.; and that no motion to adjourn prior to said hours of 4 and 10, P. M., shall be in order, if objection be made; and that on Thursday next, at 12 o'clock, noon, all debate shall cease, and the Convention proceed to vote upon the questions or propositions before them in their order.

After debate, the whole subject was, on motion of Mr. Morehead, of North Carolina, laid upon the table until 10 o'clock, A. M., to-morrow.

Mr. Ruffin, of North Carolina, gave notice of his intention to offer certain amendments to the majority report of the committee.

A motion was made that when this Convention adjourns it adjourn to meet at ten o'clock, A. M. An amendment was offered to insert *half-past ten*. A further amendment was proposed to adjourn to half-past seven this P. M. The resolution and amendments were subsequently withdrawn; whereupon the motion to adjourn to ten o'clock, A. M., was renewed. pending a vote upon which a motion was made to adjourn, and declared carried.

WASHINGTON CITY, *February* 20, 1861.

Convention met at ten o'clock.

President Tyler in the chair.

After prayer by the Rev. Dr. Samson, the journal of yesterday was read and approved.

Mr. Harris, of Vermont, offered the following preamble and resolutions; which were read, ordered to be printed, and laid on the table:

WHEREAS, The Federal Constitution, and the laws made in pursuance thereof, are the supreme law of the land, and should command the willing obedience of all good citizens; and whereas, it is alleged that sundry States have enacted laws repugnant thereto; therefore,

Resolved, That this Convention respectfully requests the several States to revise their respective enactments, and to modify or repeal any laws which may be found to be in conflict with the Constitution and laws of the United States.

Resolved, That the President of this Convention is requested to send a copy of the foregoing preamble and resolution to the Governor of each of the States, with the request that the same be communicated to the Legislature thereof.

Mr. Randolph called up the resolutions yesterday laid upon the table, and the question was taken on striking out the latter clause of Mr. Randolph's substitute for Mr. Wickliffe's resolution, and the amendments offered thereto. A vote by States was ordered and taken, with the following result :

AYES—Connecticut, Illinois, Indiana, Iowa, Maine, Massachusetts, Maryland, New York, New Hampshire, Ohio, Pennsylvania and Vermont—12.

NOES—Delaware, Kentucky, Missouri, New Jersey, North Carolina, Rhode Island, Tennessee, and Virginia—8.

So the clause was stricken out.

Mr. Clay moved to lay the original and amendments upon the table. A vote by States being called for by Mr. Chase, resulted as follows :

AYES—Connecticut, Illinois, Indiana, Iowa, Maine, Massachusetts, New York, New Hampshire, Vermont, Virginia—10.

NOES—Delaware, Maryland, Missouri, New Jersey, North Carolina, Ohio, Pennsylvania, Rhode Island, Tennessee—9.

The resolution and amendments were laid on the table.

Mr. Wickliffe gave notice of his intention to move, on Thursday, to close the debate on the report of the Committee on Propositions and Resolutions from and after the 21st, in order to take a vote on the 22d, the birth-day of Washington.

The Convention proceeded to consider the report of the Committee on Propositions and Resolutions.

Mr. Smith, of New York, having the floor, gave way to a motion to adjourn.

Adjourned to ten o'clock, February 21.

WASHINGTON CITY, *February* 21, 1861.

Convention met pursuant to adjournment.

President Tyler in the chair.

The Convention was opened by prayer from the Rev. Mr. Stockton.

The journal was read and approved.

Mr. Chase, of Ohio, presented the following resolutions, which were read, ordered to be printed, and laid upon the table:

Resolved, That it is inexpedient to proceed to final action on the grave and important matters involved in the resolutions of the State of Virginia, in compliance with which this Convention has assembled, and in the several reports of the majority and minorities of the committee to which said resolutions were referred, until opportunity has been given to all the States to participate in deliberation and action upon them, and ample time has been allowed for such deliberation and action.

Resolved, therefore, That this Convention adjourn to meet in the City of Washington on the 4th day of April next; and that the President be requested to address a letter to the Governors of the several States not now represented in this body, urging the appointment and attendance of commissioners.

Mr. Wickliffe, pursuant to his motion of yesterday, offered and asked the adoption of the following resolutions:

Resolved, 1st. That at one o'clock, the 22d February, 1861, all debate upon the report of the committee of one from each State shall cease, and the Convention will proceed to vote, and continue to vote until the whole subject shall have been disposed of.

2d. If an amendment be offered by the commissioners of any State, or minority of such commissioners, five minutes is allowed for explanation, and the like time is allowed to the committee to resist the amendment, if they desire to do so, and the mover of the amendment, or any member of the same State, may have five minutes for reply.

3d. A motion to strike out and insert shall not be divided.

Which several resolutions were agreed to.

Mr. Dent, of Maryland, offered and asked the adoption of the following rule:

When the vote on any question is taken by States, any Commissioner dissenting from the vote of his State may have his dissent entered on the Journal.

Mr. Chase, of Ohio, offered the following as a substitute for Mr. Dent's rule:

The yeas and nays of the Commissioners of each State, upon any question, shall be entered upon the Journal when it is desired by any Commissioner, and the vote of each State shall be determined by the majority of Commissioners present from each State.

The question being upon the adoption of the substitute, the same was rejected.

The question recurring upon the original rule of Mr. Dent, it was adopted.

Mr. Bronson, of New York, moved that this Convention have a night session, and that when the Convention adjourn it shall adjourn to half-past seven o'clock this evening.

Mr. Chase called for a vote by States as to a night session, which resulted as follows:

AYES—Delaware, Illinois, Kentucky, Maryland, Missouri, New Jersey, New York, North Carolina, New Hampshire, Pennsylvania, Rhode Island, Tennessee, Virginia—13.

NOES—Connecticut, Indiana, Iowa, Maine, Massachusetts, Ohio, Vermont—7.

So the motion was carried.

Mr. Wilmot, of Pennsylvania, gave notice he should offer an amendment, as follows, to the report of the Committee on Propositions and Resolutions; which was read, laid on the table, and ordered to be printed:

And Congress shall further provide by law, that the United States shall make full compensation to a citizen of any State, who in any other State shall suffer, by reason of violence or intimidation from mobs and riotous assemblies, in his person or property, or in the deprivation by violence, of his rights secured by this Constitution.

Mr. Coulter, of Missouri, gave notice that he should offer, as an amendment to the same report, the following; which was read, laid on the table, and ordered to be printed:

The term of office of all Presidents and Vice Presidents of the United States, hereafter elected, shall be six years; and any person once elected to either of said offices, shall ever after be ineligible to the same office.

Mr. Bronson, of New York, gave notice that he should offer, as an amendment to the same report. the following; which was read, laid on the table, and ordered to be printed:

Congress shall have no power to legislate in respect to persons held to service or labor in any case, except to provide for the rendition of fugitives from such service or labor, and to suppress the foreign slave trade; and the existing status or condition of all the Territories of the United States, in respect to persons held to service or labor, shall remain unchanged during their territorial condition; and whenever any Territory, with suitable boundaries, shall contain the population requisite for a representative in Congress, according to the then federal ratio of representation, it shall be entitled to admission into the Union on an equal footing with the original States, with or without persons held to service or labor, as the Constitution of such new State may prescribe.

Mr. Hitchcock, of Ohio, gave notice that he should offer, as an amendment to the same report, the following; which was laid on the table, and ordered to be printed:

Strike out Section 3, and insert the three following:

SECTION 3. The Congress shall have no power to regulate, abolish, or control within any State the relations established or recognized by the laws thereof, touching persons held to service or labor therein.

SECTION 4. The Congress shall have no power to discharge any person held to service or labor from such service or labor in the District of Columbia, under the laws thereof, or to impair any rights pertaining to that relation under the laws now in force within the said District, without the consent of the State of Maryland, and of those to whom the service or labor is due, or making to them just compensation therefor; nor the power to interfere with or prohibit members of Congress, and officers of the Federal Government, whose duties require them to be in said District, from bringing with them, retaining, and taking away persons so held to service or labor; nor the power to impair or abolish the relations of persons owing service or labor in places under the exclusive jurisdiction of the United States, within those States and Territories where such relations are established or recognized by law.

SECTION 5. The Congress shall have no power to prohibit the removal or transportation, by land, sea, or river, of persons held to labor or service in any State or Territory of the United States, to any State or Territory thereof, where the same obligation to labor or service is established or recognized by law; and the right during such transportation of touching at ports, shores, and landings, and of landing in case of distress, shall exist; nor shall the Congress have power to authorize any higher rate of taxation on persons held to service or labor than on land.

Strike out Section 7, and insert—

SECTION 9. The Congress shall provide by law, that in all cases where the marshal, or other officer, whose duty it shall be to arrest any fugitive from service or labor, shall be prevented from so doing by violence of a mob or riotous assemblage; or where, after arrest, such fugitive shall be rescued by force, and the party to whom such service or labor is due, shall thereby be deprived of the same, the United States shall pay to such party the full value of such service or labor.

The Convention proceeded to the consideration of the report of the Committee on Propositions and Resolutions.

At half-past four, Mr. Chittenden having the floor, gave way to a motion to adjourn.

The Convention adjourned to half-past seven o'clock P. M., February 21st.

EVENING SESSION.

Convention met pursuant to adjournment at seven and a half o'clock P. M.

The Convention proceeded to the consideration of the report of the Committee on Propositions and Resolutions.

At twelve o'clock Mr. Pollock, of Pennsylvania, gave way to a motion to adjourn.

The Convention adjourned to ten o'clock A. M., February 22.

WASHINGTON CITY, *February* 22, 1861.

Convention met pursuant to adjournment. President Tyler in the chair.

Convention opened by prayer.

The journal of proceedings was read and approved.

On motion of Mr. Wickliffe, the President was authorized to appoint a committee of three upon the subject of finance and printing.

The President appointed as such committee : Mr. Johnson, of Maryland; Mr. Pollock, of Pennsylvania ; and Mr. Granger, of New York.

Mr. Turner, of Illinois, offered and moved the adoption of the following :

Resolved, That the time fixed upon to commence voting upon the questions before this Convention be postponed until Monday, February 25th, at 12 o'clock M.

A motion to lay the resolution on the table was lost by the following vote :

Ayes—Delaware, Kentucky, Maryland, Missouri, New Jersey, North Carolina, Pennsylvania, Rhode Island, Tennessee, and Virginia—10.

Noes—Connecticut, Illinois, Indiana, Iowa, Maine, Massachusetts, New York, New Hampshire, Ohio, and Vermont—10.

The resolution was withdrawn, and Mr. Chase, of Ohio, offered the same resolution.

Mr. Backus, of Ohio, offered the following substitute :

Resolved, That the resolution heretofore passed, limiting debate on amendments that shall be offered to the report of the Grand Committee, be so amended as to allow the delegates who may desire to speak not exceeding ten minutes on each amendment.

Mr. Chase accepted this in substitution of his own.

A motion by Mr. Wickliffe to lay on the table resulted in the following vote :

Ayes—Delaware, Kentucky, Maryland, Missouri, New Jersey, North Carolina, Rhode Island, Tennessee, and Virginia—9.

Noes—Connecticut, Illinois, Indiana, Iowa, Maine, Massachusetts, New York, New Hampshire, Ohio, Pennsylvania, and Vermont—11.

The Convention refused to lay on the table.

The question recurring as to the adoption of said resolution, the same prevailed by the following vote.

Ayes—Connecticut, Illinois, Indiana, Iowa, Maine, Massachusetts, New York, New Hampshire, Ohio, Pennsylvania, and Vermont—11.

Noes—Delaware, Kentucky, Maryland, Missouri, New Jersey, North Carolina, Rhode Island, Tennessee, Virginia—9.

Mr. Summers, from the Committee on Credentials, reported that the credential of J. C. Stone, as delegate from Kansas, had been duly submitted to them, examined, and approved, and he was reported as a delegate from that State.

The order of the day being the report of the Committee on Propositions and Resolutions, the Convention proceeded to the consideration of the same during the time allotted.

Mr. Field, of New York, rose to a question of privilege in regard to the adoption of the report of the Committee on Credentials, admitting the member from Kansas.

Mr. F. suggested that he was informed that the credential was issued by those not authorized to do so.

Mr. F. moved a reconsideration of the agreement to said report.

The motion was carried by the following vote:

Ayes—Delaware, Kentucky, Maryland, Missouri, New Jersey, North Carolina, Pennsylvania, Rhode Island, Tennessee, Virginia—10.

Noes—Connecticut, Illinois, Indiana, Maine Massachusetts, New York, New Hampshire, Ohio, Vermont—9.

By general consent the delegate from Iowa was asked to make his own statement as to the authenticity of said instrument.

Mr. Stone stated that the credential was regularly issued, and the authorities who executed the same were, under the Constitution of Kansas, the proper authorities; that neither the instrument nor the appointment had been questioned.

Mr. Field, of New York, moved the adoption of the following:

Resolved, That the credentials of Mr. Stone, who desires to act as a Commissioner from Kansas, be referred back to the Committee on Credentials, to report the facts concerning his appointment, and whether it proceeded from the Territorial Secretary.

Which resolution was carried.

According to previous order, the Convention proceeded to consider and vote on the report of the committee of one from each State, as submitted by Mr. Guthrie, and the amendment submitted.

The question being on the adoption of the first section of said report, as follows:

ARTICLE XIII.

Section 1. In all the present territory of the United States, not embraced within the limits of the Cherokee treaty grant, north of a line from east to west on the parallel of 36 degrees 30 minutes north latitude, involuntary servitude, except in punishment of crime, is prohibited whilst it shall be under a territorial government; and in all the present territory south of said line, the status of persons owing service or labor as it now exists shall not be changed by law while such territory shall be under a territorial government; and neither Congress nor the territorial government shall have power to hinder or prevent the taking to said territory of persons held to labor or involuntary service, within the United States, according to the laws or usages of the State from which such persons may be taken, nor to impair the rights arising out of said relations, which shall be subject to judicial cognizance in the federal courts, according to the common law; and when any territory north or south of said line, within such boundary as Congress may prescribe, shall contain a population required for a member of Congress, according to the then federal ratio of representation, it shall, if its form of government be republican, be admitted into the Union on an equal footing with the original States, with or without involuntary service or labor, as the constitution of such new State may provide.

Section 2. Territory shall not be acquired by the United States, unless by treaty; nor, except for naval and commercial stations and depots, unless such treaty shall be ratified by four fifths of all the members of the Senate.

Section 3. Neither the Constitution nor any amendment thereof shall be construed to give Congress power to regulate, abolish, or control, within any State or Territory of the United States, the relation established, or recognized by the laws thereof touching persons bound to labor or involuntary service therein; nor to interfere with or abolish involuntary service in the District of Columbia, without the consent of Maryland and without the consent of the owners, or making the owners who do not consent just compensation; nor the power to interfere with or prohibit representatives and others from bringing with them to the city of Washington, retaining and taking away, persons so bound to labor; nor the power to interfere with or abolish involuntary service in places under the exclusive jurisdiction of the United States within those States and Territories where the same is established or recognized; nor the power to prohibit the removal or transportation, by land, sea, or river, of persons held to labor or involuntary service in any State or Territory of the United States to any other State or Territory thereof where it is established or recognized by law or usage; and the right during transportation of touching at ports, shores, and landings, and of landing in case of distress, shall exist. Nor shall Congress have power to authorize any higher rate of taxation on persons bound to labor than on land.

Section 4. The third paragraph of the second section of the fourth article of the Constitution shall not be construed to prevent any of the States, by appropriate legislation, and through the action of their judicial and ministerial officers, from enforcing the delivery of fugitives from labor to the person to whom such service or labor is due.

Section 5. The foreign slave trade and the importation of slaves into the United States and their Territories, from places beyond the present limits thereof, are forever prohibited.

Section 6. The first, third, and fifth sections, together with this section six of these amendments, and the third paragraph of the second section of the first article of the Constitution, and the third paragraph of the second section of the fourth article thereof, shall not be amended or abolished without the consent of all the States.

Section 7. Congress shall provide by law that the United States shall pay to the owner the full value of his fugitive from labor, in all cases where the marshal, or other officer, whose duty it was to arrest such fugitive, was prevented from so doing by violence or intimidation from mobs or riotous assemblages, or when, after arrest, such fugitive was rescued by force, and the owner thereby prevented and obstructed in the pursuit of his remedy for the recovery of such fugitive.

Mr. Seddon, of Virginia, moved to amend the 1st section of said report by inserting after the word *line*, in clause "and in all the present territory south of said line," found in the 5th line, the following words, "including the Cherokee grant."

Mr. Fowler, of New Hampshire, moved to amend the amendment of Mr. Seddon, by substituting the word *excluding* for *including*, which prevailed by the following vote:

Ayes—Connecticut, Illinois, Indiana, Iowa, Maine, Massachusetts, New York, New Hampshire, Ohio, Pennsylvania, Vermont—11.
Noes—Delaware, Kentucky, Maryland, Missouri, New Jersey, North Carolina, Rhode Island, Tennessee, Virginia—9.

The question recurring on the adoption of the amendment of Mr. Seddon, as amended, the same was lost by the following vote:

Ayes—Connecticut, Illinois, Indiana, Iowa, Maine, Massachusetts, New York, New Hampshire, Ohio, and Vermont—10.
Noes—Delaware, Kentucky, Maryland, Missouri, New Jersey, North Carolina, Pennsylvania, Rhode Island, Tennessee, and Virginia—10.

The question recurring as to the adoption of the original report—

Mr. Reid, of North Carolina, moved to amend said first section, in the seventh line, by inserting after the word "line," at the end of the clause, "and in all the present territory south of said line," the words, "involuntary servitude is recognized, and property in those of the African race held to service or labor in any of the States of the Union, when removed to such territory shall be protected, and"—which amendment was lost by the following vote:

Ayes—Virginia, North Carolina, and Missouri—3.
Noes—Maine, New Hampshire, Vermont, Massachusetts, Rhode Island, Connecticut, New York, New Jersey, Pennsylvania, Delaware, Maryland, Tennessee, Kentucky, Ohio, Indiana, Illinois, and Iowa—17.

The following gentlemen, dissenting from the vote of their States, asked to have their names recorded as voting: Mr. Clay and Mr. Butler, of Kentucky, and Mr. Dent, Maryland, aye.

The question recurring on the original section as reported, Mr. Franklin, of Pennsylvania, moved to amend the first section by striking out therefrom all after the words "United States" in the first line, and insert in place thereof—

"Not embraced by the Cherokee treaty, north of the parallel of thirty-six degrees and thirty minutes of north latitude, involuntary servitude, except in punishment of crime, is prohibited. In all the present territory south of that line, the status of persons held to service or labor, as it now exists, shall not be changed; nor shall any law be passed to hinder or prevent the taking of such persons to said territory, nor to impair the rights arising from said relation; but the same shall be subject to judicial cognizance in the federal courts, according to the common law.

7

When any territory north or south of said line, within such boundary as Congress may prescribe, shall contain a population equal to that required for a member of Congress, it shall, if its form of government be republican, be admitted into the Union on an equal footing with the original States, with or without involuntary servitude, as the constitution of such State may provide."

Mr. Curtis, of Iowa, moved to amend the amendment of Mr. Franklin by striking out all after the word "prohibited," (found in the third line,) down to, and including, the words "common law," (found in the eighth line,) and inserting in the place thereof, "but this restriction shall not apply to territory now held south of that line."

Pending the consideration of which, the Convention adjourned to ten o'clock, the 23d of February.

WASHINGTON CITY, *February* 23*d*, 1861.

Convention met pursuant to adjournment.

President Tyler in the chair.

The proceedings were opened by prayer from the Rev. Dr. Butler.

Mr. Vandever, of Iowa, offered and moved the adoption of the following:

Resolved, That whatever may be the ultimate determination upon the amendments of the Federal Constitution, or other propositions for adjustment approved by this Convention, we, the members, do recommend our respective States and constituencies to faithfully abide in the Union.

It was moved to lay the resolution on the table, and resulted in the following vote:

AYES—Rhode Island, New Jersey, Pennsylvania, Delaware, Maryland, Virginia, North Carolina, Tennessee, Kentucky, Missouri, Ohio—11.

NOES—Maine, New Hampshire, Vermont, Massachusetts, Connecticut, New York, Indiana, Illinois, Iowa—9.

So the resolution was laid on the table.

The Convention proceeded to the consideration of the order of the day, being Mr. Curtis' amendment to Mr. Franklin's amendment to the first section of the report of the Committee on Propositions and Resolutions.

The question on the adoption of said amendment of Mr. Curtis to strike out and insert, being taken, resulted in the following vote:

AYES—Maine, Vermont, Massachusetts, Connecticut, New York, Iowa—6.

NOES—New Hampshire, Rhode Island, New Jersey, Pennsylvania, Delaware, Maryland, Virginia, North Carolina, Tennessee, Kentucky, Missouri, Ohio—12.

So the amendment was not agreed to.

The following gentlemen dissented from the vote of their States:

Amos Tuck, of New Hampshire.
Erastus Corning, of New York.
Francis Granger, of New York.
Greene C. Bronson, of New York.
William E. Dodge, of New York.
David Wilmot, of Pennsylvania.
C. P. Wolcott, of Ohio.

Mr. Bronson moved the adoption of the following:

Resolved, Whereas, John E. Wool, a delegate from New York, is unable to attend the Convention from sickness, therefore, that he be permitted, when he does attend, or by communication to the Secretary in writing, to have his dissent recorded as to any vote of his State.

Agreed to unanimously.

The question recurring as to the adoption of the amendment of Mr. Franklin :

The following amendments were proposed and accepted by Mr. Franklin :

1st. In the 5th line, after the word *passed*, (occurring in the clause, "nor shall any law be passed,") insert the words, "by Congress or the Territorial Legislature."

2d. In the 6th line, after the word "persons," (occurring in the clause, "the taking of such persons,") insert, "from any of the States of this Union."

3d. In the 8th line, before the words "common law," (occurring in the clause, "according to the common law,") insert the words "course of the."

Mr. James moved to amend Mr. Franklin's amended proposition, in the 5th line, by inserting the words "nor facilitate," after the word "prevent," (occurring in the clause, "to hinder or prevent.")

The question, on agreeing to said amendment, resulted in the following vote :

Ayes—Maine, New Hampshire, Vermont, Massachusetts, Rhode Island, Connecticut, New York, Indiana, Illinois, Iowa—9.

Noes—New Jersey, Pennsylvania, Delaware, Maryland, Virginia, North Carolina, Tennessee, Kentucky, Missouri, Ohio—10.

So the amendment was not agreed to.

Mr. Wilmot moved to amend Mr. Franklin's proposition, in the 4th line, by inserting the word "legal" before the word "status," (occurring in the clause, "the status of persons held to service.")

The question on agreeing to said amendment resulted in the following vote :

Ayes—Maine, New Hampshire, Vermont, Massachusetts, Connecticut, New York, Indiana Illinois, Iowa—9.

Noes—Rhode Island, New Jersey, Pennsylvania, Delaware, Maryland, Virginia, North Carolina, Tennessee, Kentucky, Missouri, Ohio—11.

So the amendment was not agreed to.

Mr. Turner moved to amend Mr. Franklin's amendment in the 5th line, by inserting the word "encourage" after the word "prevent," (occurring in the clause, "hinder or prevent the taking of such persons.")

The question on agreeing to said amendment resulted in the following vote :

Ayes—Maine, New Hampshire, Vermont, Massachusetts, Rhode Island, Connecticut, New York, Indiana, Illinois, Iowa—10

Noes—New Jersey, Pennsylvania, Delaware, Maryland, Virginia, North Carolina, Tennessee, Kentucky, Missouri, Ohio—10.

So the amendment was not agreed to.

Mr. Goodrich, of Massachusetts, moved to amend Mr. Franklin's amendment, by striking out from the first line, the words following: "not embraced by the Cherokee treaty."

The question on agreeing to said amendment resulted in the following vote :

Ayes—Maine, New Hampshire, Vermont, Massachusetts, Connecticut, New York, Pennsylvania, Ohio, Indiana, Illinois, Iowa—11.

Noes—Rhode Island, New Jersey, Delaware, Maryland, Virginia, North Carolina, Tennessee, Kentucky, Missouri—9.

So the amendment was agreed to.

Mr. Seddon, in behalf of President Tyler, moved to amend the amendment of Mr. Franklin, by inserting at the close of said amendment, so as to follow after the clause relating to division of territory, the following :

All appointments to office in the territories lying north of the line 36 degrees and 30 minutes, as well before as after the establishment of Territorial governments in and over the same, or any part thereof, shall be made upon the recommendation of a majority of the Senators representing at the time the non-slaveholding States. And in like manner, all appointments to office in the territories which may lie south of said line of 36 degrees and 30 minutes shall be made upon the recommendation of a majority of the Senators representing at the time the slaveholding States. But nothing in this article shall be construed to restrain the President of the United States from removing, for actual incompetency or misdemeanor in office, any person thus appointed, and appointing a temporary agent, to be continued in office until the majority of Senators as aforesaid may present a new recommendation, or from filling any vacancy which may occur during the recess of the Senate, such appointment to continue *ad interim*. And to insure on the part of the Senators the selection of the most trustworthy agents, it is hereby directed that all the net proceeds arising from the sales of the public lands shall be distributed annually among the several States, according to the combined ratio of representation and taxation; but the distribution aforesaid may be suspended by Congress in case of actual war with a foreign nation, or imminent peril thereof.

By unanimous consent, the rule was suspended in reference to the ten minute rule in behalf of Mr. Tyler, (President,) who proposed to address the Convention.

The question on agreeing to the proposed amendment of Mr. Seddon, was, on motion, divided, and the vote on the first part resulted as follows:

AYES—Maryland, Virginia, North Carolina, Kentucky, Missouri—5.
NOES—Maine, New Hampshire, Vermont, Massachusetts, Rhode Island, Connecticut, New York, New Jersey, Pennsylvania, Tennessee, Ohio, Indiana, Illinois, Iowa—14.

So the first part of the proposed amendment was not agreed to. The second part was withdrawn.

The following gentlemen dissented from the vote of their State:
Reverdy Johnson, of Maryland.
Jno. W. Crisfield, of Maryland.

Mr. McCurdy moved to amend the amendment of Mr. Franklin, by adding at the end thereof the words following:

Provided, That nothing in this article shall be so construed as to carry any law of involuntary servitude into such Territory.

The question on agreeing to said amendment resulted in the following vote:

AYES—Maine, New Hampshire, Vermont, Massachusetts, Connecticut, New York, Iowa—7
NOES—Rhode Island, New Jersey, Pennsylvania, Delaware, Maryland, Virginia, North Carolina, Tennessee, Kentucky, Missouri, Ohio, Indiana, Illinois—13.

So the amendment was not agreed to.

The following gentleman dissented from the vote of his State:
Mr. Orth, of Indiana.

Mr. Chase moved that the Convention adjourn to Monday.

The question on agreeing to said motion resulted in the following vote:

AYES—Maine, Massachusetts, Connecticut, New York, Indiana—5
NOES—New Hampshire, Vermont, Rhode Island, New Jersey, Pennsylvania, Delaware, Maryland, Virginia, North Carolina, Tennessee, Kentucky, Missouri—12.

So the Convention refused to adjourn.

The question recurring on Mr. Franklin's amendment as amended, was determined by the following vote:

AYES—Maine, New Hampshire, Vermont, Rhode Island, Connecticut, New York, New Jersey, Pennsylvania, Delaware, Maryland, Kentucky, Ohio, Indiana, Illinois—14.
NOES—Virginia, North Carolina, Tennessee, Missouri—4.

So the amendment of Mr. Franklin was agreed to.

It was agreed unanimously, that President Tyler inform the Hon. A. Lincoln, (President elect of the United States,) that the members of this Convention would be happy to wait upon him at such time as would suit his convenience, and that the President inform this Convention of the result.

On motion of Mr. Logan, the Convention adjourned to 7½ P. M., February 23.

SATURDAY EVENING, 7½ O'CLOCK.

The Convention met pursuant to adjournment.

Mr. Summers, from the Committee on Credentials, to whom was recommitted the report of said committee, as to J. C. Stone as a delegate from Kansas, reported the same back without amendment, and recommended the admission of said member; which was agreed to.

Mr. Summers, from the same committee, made a further report, that the credentials of the gentlemen hereafter named had been duly submitted to and examined by said committee, and were approved by them, and they reported and recommended them to be admitted as delegates:

      M. F. Conway, from Kansas.

      Henry J. Adams, from Kansas.

      Thos. Ewing, jr., from Kansas.

Which was agreed to.

The Convention proceeded to the consideration of the order of the day, being the adoption of the 2d section of the report of Mr. Guthrie, from the Committee on Propositions, &c.

Mr. Summers, of Virginia, moved the adoption of the following as an amendment: To strike out all of said section, and in place thereof, insert

No territory shall be acquired by the United States without the concurrence of a majority of all the Senators from States which allow involuntary servitude, and a majority of all the Senators from States which prohibit that relation; nor shall territory be acquired by treaty, unless the votes of a majority of the Senators from each class of States hereinbefore mentioned, be cast as a part of the two-third majority necessary to the ratification of such treaty.

Mr. Johnson, of Maryland, moved to amend the same by inserting, after the words "United States," in the first line, the words, "except by discovery, and for naval and commercial stations, depots, and transit routes."

Which was accepted by Mr. Summers.

The question on the adoption of said amendment of Mr. Summers resulted in the following vote:

AYES—Rhode Island, New Jersey, Delaware, Maryland, Virginia, North Carolina, Tennessee, Kentucky, Missouri—9.

NOES—Maine, Vermont, Massachusetts, Connecticut, New York, Pennsylvania, Indiana, Illinois. Iowa, Kansas—10.

So the amendment was not agreed to.

Mr. Guthrie, of Kentucky, moved the adoption of the following as an amendment; to strike out the second section, and substitute in place the following:

"Territory may be acquired for naval and commercial stations, depots, and transit routes, and by discovery, and for no other purposes, without the concurrence of four fifths of the Senate."

The question on the adoption of Mr. Guthrie's amendment resulted in the following vote:

AYES—New Hampshire, Rhode Island, Connecticut, New Jersey, Pennsylvania, Delaware, Maryland, Tennessee, Kentucky, Ohio—10.

NOES—Maine, Vermont, Massachusetts, New York, Virginia, North Carolina, Missouri, Indiana, Illinois, Iowa—10.

So the amendment was not agreed to.

The following gentleman dissented from the vote of his State:

R. M. Price, of New Jersey.

Moved that the order of the day be suspended, in order to hear the report of the President in regard to the reception of Mr. Lincoln, the President elect.

Mr. Tyler informed the Convention that he had, according to request, communicated with Mr. Lincoln, the President elect, and that at nine o'clock, or any time thereafter, he would be happy to receive the members of the Convention.

Mr. Wickliffe, of Kentucky, moved that a committee of three be appointed by the President to make arrangements for the reception of the members of the Convention.

The President appointed as such committee:

Mr. Wickliffe, of Kentucky; Mr. Field, of New York; Mr. Chase, of Ohio.

Mr. McKennan, of Pennsylvania, moved a reconsideration of the vote on the amendment of Mr. Summers.

Pending which, the proceedings were suspended to hear the report of the committee to arrange for the reception of the members of the Convention by Mr. Lincoln, the President elect.

Mr. Field, in behalf of said committee, reported that Mr. Lincoln was *then* desirous of receiving the members of the Convention, at his parlor.

Mr. Ewing moved that the Convention adjourn to Monday, at 10 o'clock, A. M.

WASHINGTON CITY, *February* 25, 1861.

The Convention met pursuant to adjournment. President Tyler in the chair.

The proceedings were opened by prayer from the Rev. Mr. Smith.

The journal of the 23d was read and approved.

Mr. Hackleman, on behalf of Indiana, asked to record the vote of that State on the amendment of Mr. Curtis, voted on on the 23d inst.

Leave was granted. Voted: recorded as of that day.

The President informed the Convention that he had received certain resolutions, purporting to emanate from the Democratic State Convention of Pennsylvania, which he was asked to present, which he accordingly did, and requested to know what action the Convention would take on the same.

Mr. Clay, of Kentucky, stated, that as the Convention had not received or acted on any mere party proposition, he moved to lay the proceedings on the table.

Which was agreed to.

Mr. Brockenbrough, of Virginia, presented certain amendments, which he proposed to offer at the proper time, and which he read and asked to have printed.

(These have not been sent to the Secretary.)

The order of the day being the reconsideration of the vote taken on the 23d on the amendment proposed by Mr. Summers, the same, by general consent, was passed informally for the present, subject to call.

The Convention proceeded to the consideration of the third section of Mr. Guthrie's report.

Mr. Guthrie moved to amend said report, in the 13th line of this report, by striking out the words, "by land, sea, or river."

Which was agreed to.

Mr. Guthrie moved to amend the same section, in the 16th line of this journal, after the word "transportation," and insert "by sea or river."

Which was agreed to.

Mr. Hitchcock, of Ohio, moved to amend said section by striking out all after the word "give," in the 2d line of this journal, and insert:

Strike out Section 3, and insert the three following:

SECTION 3. Neither the Constitution, nor any amendment thereof, shall be construed to give to Congress power to regulate, abolish, or control, within any State, the relations established or recognized by the laws thereof, touching persons held to service or labor therein.

SECTION 4. Congress shall have no power to discharge any person held to service or labor in the District of Columbia, under the laws thereof, from such service or labor, or to impair any rights pertaining to that relation under the laws now in force within the said District, while such relation shall exist in the State of Maryland, without the consent of said State, and of those to whom the service or labor is due, or making to them just compensation therefor ; nor the power to interfere with, or prohibit, members of Congress, and officers of the Federal Government, whose duties require them to be in said District, from bringing with them, for personal service only, retaining, and taking away persons so held to service or labor ; nor the power to impair or abolish the relations of persons owing service or labor in places under the exclusive jurisdiction of the United States, within those States and Territories where such relations are established or recognized by law.

SECTION 5. Congress shall have no power to prohibit the removal or transportation of persons held to labor or service in any State or Territory of the United States, to any State or Territory thereof, where the same obligation or liability to labor or service is established or recognized by law ; and the right during such transportation, by sea or river, of touching at ports, shores, and landings, and of landing in case of distress, shall exist ; nor shall the Congress have power to authorize any higher rate of taxation on persons held to service or labor than on land.

Strike out Section 7, and insert—

SECTION 9. Congress shall provide by law, that in all cases where the marshal, or other officer, whose duty it shall be to arrest any fugitive from service or labor, shall be prevented from so doing by violence of a mob or riotous assemblage, or where, after arrest, such fugitive shall be rescued by like violence, and the party to whom such service or labor is due shall thereby be deprived of the same, the United States shall pay to such party the full value of such service or labor.

Mr. James moved to amend the amendment of Mr. Hitchcock by striking out, and inserting:

1st. No amendment shall be made to the Constitution which will authorize or give to Congress the power to abolish or interfere, within any State, with the domestic institutions thereof, including that of persons held to labor or service by the laws of said State.

The question on the adoption of said amendment resulted in the following vote:

AYES—Maine, New Hampshire, Vermont, Massachusetts, Connecticut, New York, Indiana—7.

NOES—Rhode Island, New Jersey, Pennsylvania, Delaware, Maryland, Virginia, North Carolina, Tennessee, Kentucky, Missouri, Ohio, Illinois, Kansas—13.

So the amendment was not agreed to.

Mr. Wood dissented from the vote of his State.

Mr. Baldwin moved to amend the amendment of Mr. Hitchcock by striking out the words, "nor shall Congress have the power to authorize any higher rate of taxation on persons held to service or labor than on land."

Mr. H. withdrew his proposed amendment for the present.

Mr. Seddon moved to amend the third section of the original report in the third line, by inserting after the word "State," the words, "obstruct, hinder, or prevent."

The question on the adoption of this amendment resulted in the following vote :

Ayes—Maryland, Virginia, North Carolina, Tennessee, Kentucky, Missouri—6.
Noes—Maine, New Hampshire, Vermont, Massachusetts, Rhode Island, Connecticut, New York, New Jersey, Pennsylvania, Delaware, Ohio, Indiana, Illinois, Kentucky—14.

So the amendment was not agreed to.

Mr. Seddon moved to amend the third section of the report by striking out the "City of Washington," in the ninth line, (this report,) and insert "District of Columbia."

Which was agreed to.

Mr. Seddon offered to amend the third section of the report by inserting the words "and Virginia," after the words "District of Columbia," in the ninth line, (of this report,) as substituted as per last agreement.

The question on agreeing to said amendment resulted in the following vote :

Ayes—Maryland, Virginia, North Carolina, Tennessee, Missouri—5.
Noes—Maine, New Hampshire, Vermont, Massachusetts, Rhode Island, Connecticut, New York, New Jersey, Pennsylvania, Kentucky, Ohio, Indiana, Illinois, Kansas—14.

So the amendment was not agreed to.

Mr. Seddon moved to amend the third section by inserting after the word "exist," in the seventeenth line (of this report,) these words : "And if the transportation be by sea, the right of property in the person held to service or labor shall be protected by the Federal Government as other property."

The question on agreeing to said amendment resulted in the following vote :

Ayes—Virginia, North Carolina, Tennessee, Missouri—4.
Noes—Maine, New Hampshire, Vermont, Massachusetts, Rhode Island, Connecticut, New York, New Jersey, Pennsylvania, Delaware, Maryland, Kentucky, Ohio, Indiana, Illinois, Iowa, Kansas—17.

So the amendment was not agreed to.

The following gentlemen dissented from the vote of their State :

Mr. Doniphan, Mr. Johnson, of Missouri.
Mr. Dent, Mr. Crisfield, of Maryland.
Mr. Clay, Mr. Butler, of Kentucky.

Mr. Seddon moved to amend the third section by inserting after the word "exist," in the seventeenth line, as above, the following :

"And the rights of transit by persons holding those of the African race to labor or service, in and through the States not recognizing the relations of persons held to labor or service, in passing with them from one State or Territory recognizing such relations to another, shall be secure."

The question on agreeing to said amendment resulted in the following vote :

Ayes—Virginia, North Carolina, Kentucky, Missouri—4.
Noes—Maine, New Hampshire, Vermont, Massachusetts, Rhode Island, Connecticut, New York, New Jersey, Pennsylvania, Delaware, Maryland, Tennessee, Ohio, Indiana, Illinois, Iowa, Kansas—17.

So the amendment was not agreed to.

Mr. Seddon moved to amend the third section by inserting in the fourth line, (of this report,) after the word "touching," the following words : "The relations existing between master and slave."

The question on agreeing to said amendment resulted in the following vote :

Ayes—Virginia, North Carolina, Missouri—3.

Noes—Maine, New Hampshire, Vermont, Massachusetts, Rhode Island, Connecticut, New York, New Jersey, Pennsylvania, Delaware, Maryland, Tennessee, Kentucky, Ohio, Indiana, Illinois, Iowa, Kansas—18.

So the amendment was not agreed to.

The following gentlemen dissented from the vote of their State:

        Mr. Alexander, of New Jersey.
        Mr. Dent, of Maryland.
        Mr. Clay, of Kentucky.

Mr. Hall, of Vermont, moved to amend the third section of said report in the 10th line, (this report,) by striking out the word "nor," and inserting in place thereof, "but the bringing into said District of persons held to service for the purpose of being sold, or placed in depot to be afterwards transferred to any other place to be sold as merchandise, is forever prohibited, and Congress may pass all necessary laws to make this prohibition effectual; nor shall Congress have"—

The question on agreeing to said amendment resulted in the following vote:

Ayes—Maine, New Hampshire, Vermont, Massachusetts, Connecticut, New York, Ohio, Indiana, Iowa, Kansas—10.

Noes—Rhode Island, New Jersey. Pennsylvania, Delaware, Maryland, Virginia, North Carolina, Tennessee, Kentucky, Missouri—10.

So the amendment was agreed to.

The following gentlemen dissented from the vote of their State:

        Mr. Hoppin, Mr. Brown, of Rhode Island.

Mr. McCurdy, moved to amend said third section, by inserting, at the close thereof, the following words:

"Provided, that nothing in this section shall be so construed as to prevent any State in which involuntary servitude is prohibited, from restraining by law the transfer of such persons, or of any right or interest in their services, from one individual to another, within the limits of such State."

The question on the adoption of said amendment resulted in the following vote:

Ayes—Maine, New Hampshire, Vermont, Massachusetts, Connecticut, New York, Ohio, Indiana, Illinois, Iowa, Kansas—11.

Noes—Rhode Island, New Jersey, Pennsylvania, Delaware, Maryland, Virginia, North Carolina, Tennessee, Kentucky, Missouri—10.

So the amendment was agreed to.

The following gentlemen dissented from the vote of their State:

        Mr. Logan, of Illinois.
        Mr. Palmer, of Illinois.

Mr. Turner moved a reconsideration of the above vote, which was agreed to. The immediate consideration of said question was passed.

Mr. Hitchcock proposed to insist on his amendment.

Mr. Brown moved to lay the amendment of Mr. Hitchcock on the table.

Which was agreed to.

Mr. Baldwin moved to strike out all after the word "exist," in the 17th line.

Which was not agreed to.

Mr. Bates, of Delaware, moved to amend said section by striking out the word "bound," where it occurs in the 4th, 10th, 19th lines, or other places, and insert "held;" also to insert, after the word "held," the words "or service."

Which were agreed to.

8

Mr. Groesbeck moved to amend said 3d section by striking out the same, and inserting in place thereof the following:

SECTION 3. Congress shall have no power to abolish or control within any State the relations established or recognized by the laws thereof, respecting persons held to service or labor therein.

SECTION 4. Congress shall have no power to legislate respecting the relation of service or labor in places under its exclusive jurisdiction, but within States where that relation is established or recognized, and while it continues, without the consent of such States; nor abolish or impair such relation in the District of Columbia, without the consent of Maryland, and compensation to persons to whom such service or labor is due.

SECTION 5. Congress shall have no power to prohibit the removal, from any State or Territory, of persons held to service or labor therein, to any other State or Territory in which persons are so held; and the right, during removal, of touching at ports, shores, and landings, and of landing in case of distress, shall exist, but not the right of transit in or through any State or Territory without its consent. No higher rate of taxation shall be imposed on persons so held than on land.

The question on the adoption of said amendment resulted in the following vote:

AYES—New Hampshire, Rhode Island, Connecticut, Pennsylvania, Delaware, Ohio, Indiana—7.

NOES—Maine, Vermont, Massachusetts, New York, New Jersey, Maryland, Virginia, North Carolina, Tennessee, Missouri, Illinois, Kansas—12.

So the amendment was not agreed to.

Mr. Pollock moved to amend said section by inserting after the word "distress," in the 17th line of this report, " but not for sale or traffic."

Which was agreed to.

Mr. Vandever moved to amend said section by adding to the section the following:

Provided nothing herein contained shall be so construed as to prevent any State from prohibiting the introduction as merchandise of persons held to service or labor, or to prevent such State from prohibiting the transit of persons so held to service or labor through its limits.

The question on agreeing to said amendment resulted in the following vote:

AYES—Maine, Vermont, Massachusetts, Connecticut, New York, Indiana, Iowa—7.

NOES—New Hampshire, Rhode Island, New Jersey, Pennsylvania, Delaware, Maryland, Virginia, North Carolina, Tennessee, Kentucky, Missouri, Ohio, Illinois, Kansas—14.

So the amendment was not agreed to.

Mr. Clay, of Kentucky, asked unanimous consent to introduce the Crittenden propositions.

Which was not given.

Mr. Groesbeck moved to amend said third section by inserting after the word "traffic," the words, "but not the right of transit in or through any State or Territory without its consent."

Mr. Ruffin moved to amend the amendment by substituting in lieu of the words, "without its consent," the words, "against its dissent."

Which was agreed to.

The question on agreeing to the amendment of Mr. Groesbeck resulted in the following vote:

AYES—Maine, New Hampshire, Vermont, Massachusetts, Rhode Island, Connecticut, New York, New Jersey, Pennsylvania, Ohio—10.

NOES—Delaware, Maryland, Virginia, North Carolina, Tennessee, Kentucky, Missouri, Illinois—8.

So the amendment was agreed to.

The following gentleman dissented from the vote of his State:

Mr. Alexander, of New Jersey.

Mr. Granger moved that when the Convention adjourns it will adjourn to 7½ this evening.

The question on the adjournment resulted in the following vote:

AYES—Maine, New Hampshire, Vermont, Massachusetts, Connecticut, New York, Pennsylvania, Tennessee, Ohio, Indiana, Illinois, Iowa, Kansas—13.

NOES—Rhode Island, New Jersey, Delaware, Maryland, Kentucky, Missouri—6.

So the Convention agreed to adjourn to 7½, P. M.

On motion of Mr. Chase, the Convention then adjourned.

The Convention adjourned to 7½, P. M.

FEBRUARY 25, 7½, P. M.

The Convention met pursuant to adjournment.

Mr. Smith, of New York, proposed that a committee of two be appointed by the Chair to arrange for the printing of the journal.

The Chair appointed—

    Mr. Smith, of New York.

    Mr. Howard, of Maryland.

The Convention proceeded to the consideration of the order of the day, being the third section of the report.

Mr. Hitchcock moved to amend the third section by striking out the words "or territory of the United States," in the third line; also to strike out in the third and fourth lines. (this report,) the word "involuntary."

The question on agreeing to said amendment resulted in the following vote:

AYES—Maine, New Hampshire, Vermont, Massachusetts, Connecticut, New York, Pennsylvania, Ohio, Indiana, Kentucky—10.

NOES—Rhode Island, New Jersey, Delaware, Maryland, Virginia, North Carolina, Tennessee, Kentucky, Missouri—9.

So the amendments were agreed to.

Mr. Summers called up for consideration the amendment which had been proposed by him on the 23d, as amended by Mr. Johnson, to the second section, as follows:

"No territory shall be acquired by the United States, except by discovery and for naval and commercial stations, depots, and transit routes, without the concurrence of a majority of all the Senators from States which allow involuntary servitude, and a majority of all the Senators from States which prohibit that relation; nor shall territory be acquired by treaty, unless the votes of a majority of the Senators from each class of States hereinbefore mentioned be cast as a part of the two third majority necessary to the ratification of such treaty."

The question on agreeing to said amendment resulted in the following vote:

AYES—New Hampshire, Rhode Island, New Jersey, Pennsylvania, Delaware, Maryland, Virginia, North Carolina, Tennessee, Kentucky, Missouri, Ohio—12.

NOES—Maine, Massachusetts, Connecticut, Indiana, Illinois, Kansas—6.

So the amendment was agreed to.

The Convention proceeded to the consideration of the fourth section of the report. No amendments being proposed, they proceeded to the fifth section.

Mr. Seddon, of Virginia, moved to strike out all of said section.

The question on agreeing to said motion resulted in the following vote:

AYES—Virginia, North Carolina, Kentucky, Missouri—4.

NOES—Maine, New Hampshire, Vermont, Massachusetts, Rhode Island, Connecticut, New York, New Jersey, Pennsylvania, Delaware, Maryland, Tennessee, Ohio, Indiana, Illinois, Iowa, Kansas—17.

So the Convention refused to strike out.

Mr. James moved to amend said section by striking out the following words: "From places beyond the present limits thereof."

The question on agreeing to said amendment resulted in the following vote:

Ayes—Maine, New Hampshire, Vermont, Massachusetts, Rhode Island, Connecticut, New York, New Jersey, Pennsylvania, Delaware, Maryland, Tennessee, Kentucky, Ohio, Indiana, Illinois, Kansas—17.
Noes—Virginia, North Carolina, Missouri—3.

So the amendment was agreed to.

Mr. Seddon, of Virginia, moved to amend said section by inserting, in the fore part of said section, the words: "The Congress shall have power to prohibit," and to strike out from the latter clause, the words "and forever prohibit."

The question on agreeing to said amendment resulted in the following vote:

Ayes—Maryland, Virginia, North Carolina, Tennessee, Missouri—5.
Noes—Maine, New Hampshire, Vermont, Massachusetts, Rhode Island, Connecticut, New York, New Jersey, Pennsylvania, Delaware, Kentucky, Ohio, Indiana, Illinois, Iowa, Kansas—16.

So the amendment was not agreed to.

Mr. Doniphan and Mr. Johnson, of Missouri, dissent from the vote of their State.

Mr. Morehead moved to amend said section by striking out and inserting in lieu thereof:

" The foreign slave trade is hereby forever prohibited; and it shall be the duty of Congress to pass laws to prevent the importation of slaves into the United States and their Territories beyond the limits thereof."

Mr. Wickliffe, of Kentucky, moved to amend said amendment, by inserting after "importation of slaves," the words "coolies, or persons held to service or labor."

Which was accepted by Mr. Morehead.

The question on agreeing to said amendment of Mr. Morehead resulted in the following vote:

Ayes—Pennsylvania, Delaware, Maryland, Virginia, North Carolina, Tennessee, Kentucky, Missouri, Ohio, Indiana, Illinois—11.
Noes—Maine, New Hampshire, Vermont, Massachusetts, Rhode Island, New York, New Jersey, Kansas—8.

So the amendment was agreed to

The following gentlemen disagreed to the vote of their States :

Mr. Hoppin, of Rhode Island.
Mr. Orth, of Indiana.
Mr. Ellis, of Indiana.
Mr. Stockton, of New Jersey.

Mr. ——————, of Massachusetts, moved to strike out the whole section.

The question on striking out resulted in the following vote:

Ayes—Massachusetts, Virginia, Tennessee—3.
Noes—Maine, New Hampshire, Vermont, Rhode Island, Connecticut, New York, New Jersey, Pennsylvania, Delaware, Maryland, North Carolina, Kentucky, Missouri, Ohio, Indiana, Illinois, Iowa, Kansas—18.

So the Convention refused to strike out.

The Convention proceeded to the consideration of the sixth section.

No amendment being proposed, they proceeded to the seventh section.

Mr. Turner, of Illinois, moved the adoption of the following amendment to the seventh section, by striking out and inserting:

"Congress shall provide by law for securing to the citizens of each State the privileges and immunities of citizens of the several States."

Mr. Logan, of Illinois, moved to amend said amendment by inserting "free white" before the word "citizens."

The question on agreeing to said amendment resulted in the following vote:

AYES—New Jersey, Pennsylvania, Delaware, Maryland, Virginia, North Carolina, Tennessee, Kentucky, Indiana, Illinois—10.
NOES—Maine, New Hampshire, Vermont, Massachusetts, Rhode Island, Connecticut, New York, Iowa—8.

So the amendment was agreed to.

Mr. Orth, of Indiana, disagreed to the vote of his State.

The question recurring on the amendment as amended, resulted in the following vote:

AYES—None.
NOES—Maine, New Hampshire, Vermont, Massachusetts, Rhode Island, Connecticut, New York, New Jersey, Pennsylvania, Delaware, Maryland, Virginia, North Carolina, Tennessee, Kentucky, Missouri, Ohio, Indiana—18.

So the amendment was not agreed to.

Mr. Wilmot moved the adoption of the following as an amendment to the seventh section:

"And Congress shall further provide by law, that the United States shall make full compensation to a citizen of any State, who in any other State shall suffer, by reason of violence or intimidation from mobs and riotous assemblies, in his person or property, or in the deprivation, by violence, of his rights secured by this Constitution."

Mr. Orth moved that the Convention adjourn, which resulted in the following vote:

AYES—Maine, Connecticut, New York, Indiana, Illinois, Iowa, Kansas—7.
NOES—New Hampshire, Vermont, Massachusetts, Rhode Island, New Jersey, Pennsylvania, Delaware, Maryland, Virginia, North Carolina, Tennessee, Kentucky, Missouri, Ohio—14.

So the Convention refused to adjourn.

The question recurring to agree to the amendment of Mr. Wilmot, resulted in the following vote:

AYES—Maine, Vermont, Massachusetts, New York, Pennsylvania, Indiana, Illinois, Iowa—8.
NOES—Rhode Island, Connecticut, New Jersey, Delaware, Maryland, Virginia, North Carolina, Tennessee, Kentucky, Missouri, Ohio—11.

So the amendment was not agreed to.

Mr Barringer moved to amend the seventh section by adding at the end of this section the words following:

"And in all cases in which the United States shall pay for such fugitive, Congress shall also provide for the collection by the United States of the amount so paid, with interest, from the county, city, or town, in which such arrest shall have been prevented, or rescue made."

The question on agreeing to said amendment resulted in the following vote:

AYES—Virginia, North Carolina, and Kansas—3.
NOES—Maine, New Hampshire, Vermont, Massachusetts, Rhode Island, Connecticut, New York, New Jersey, Pennsylvania, Delaware, Maryland, Tennessee, Kentucky, Ohio, Indiana, Illinois, and Iowa—17.

So the amendment was not agreed to.

The following gentlemen disagreed to the vote of their States:

Mr. Kent, of Maryland.
Mr. Clay, of Kentucky.

Mr. Frelinghuysen moved to amend the 7th section by adding the following words:

"Congress shall provide by law for securing to the citizens of each State the privileges immunities of citizens in the several States."

The question on the adoption of said amendment resulted in the following vote:

AYES—Connecticut, Delaware, Illinois, Indiana, Iowa, Maine Massachusetts, Maryland, New Jersey, New York, New Hampshire, Ohio, Pennsylvania, Rhode Island Vermont, Kansas—16.
NOES—Kentucky, Missouri, North Carolina, Tennessee, Virginia—4.

So the amendment was agreed to.
The following gentleman dissented from the vote of his State:
Mr. Roman, of Maryland.

Mr. Ames, of Massachusetts, moved to amend said section by striking out the word "force," and inserting in place of the same the words: "like violence and intimidation;" which was agreed to.

Mr. Orth, of Indiana, moved to amend said section by adding at the close thereof the following words:

"And such fugitive shall then be discharged from such service, after being paid therefor."

The question on the adoption of said amendment resulted in the following vote:

AYES—Illinois, Indiana, Iowa, Maine, Massachusetts, New York, New Hampshire, Ohio, Pennsylvania, Kansas—10.
NOES—Connecticut, Delaware, Kentucky, Maryland, Missouri, New Jersey, North Carolina, Rhode Island, Tennessee, Vermont, Virginia—11.

So the amendment was not agreed to.
Mr. Clay moved to amend said report by adding as Section 8 the following:

"The second paragraph of the second section of fourth article of Constitution shall be so construed that no State shall have the power to consider and determine what is treason, felony, or crime in another State; but that a person charged in any State with treason, felony, or crime, who shall flee from justice and be found in another State, shall, on demand of the executive authority of the State from which he fled, be delivered up, to be removed to the State having jurisdiction of the crime."

The question on agreeing to said amendment resulted in the following vote:

AYES—Kentucky, Missouri, North Carolina, Tennessee, Virginia—5.
NOES—Connecticut, Delaware, Illinois, Indiana, Iowa, Maine, Massachusetts, Maryland, New Jersey, New York, New Hampshire, Ohio, Pennsylvania, Rhode Island, Vermont, Kansas—16.

So the amendment was not agreed to.
At 2 o'clock, A. M:, Convention adjourned to 11, A. M., on the 26th.

Convention met pursuant to adjournment.
The order of the day being the reconsideration of the vote on Mr. Orth's amendment,
The question as to the reconsideration of said vote resulted as follows:

AYES—Connecticut, Illinois, Indiana, Iowa, Maine, Massachusetts, New York, New Hampshire, Ohio, Vermont, Kansas—11.
NOES—Delaware, Kentucky, Maryland, Missouri, New Jersey, North Carolina, Pennsylvania, Rhode Island, Tennessee, Virginia—10.

So the vote was reconsidered.

Mr. Backus moved to amend the amendment of Mr. Orth, by substituting the following:

"And the acceptance of such payment shall preclude the owner from further claim to said fugitive."

The question on the adoption of the amendment resulted as follows:

AYES—Connecticut, Delaware, Illinois, Iowa, Kentucky, Maine, Massachusetts, Maryland, New Jersey, New York, North Carolina, New Hampshire, Ohio, Pennsylvania, Rhode Island, Tennessee, Vermont—17.

NOES—Indiana, Missouri, Virginia—3.

So the amendment was agreed to.

The following gentlemen dissented from the votes of their States:

Mr. Dent, Mr. Roman, of Maryland.

Mr. Stephens, Mr. Totten, of Tennessee.

Mr. Bronson, of New York, moved the adoption of the following:

"Before reaching the final question on the plan to be submitted to Congress, no member shall be allowed to speak more than three minutes on any proposition."

Which was laid on the table.

Mr. Field moved to amend said report by adding the following:

SECTION 8. The union of the States under the Constitution is indissoluble, and no State can secede from the Union, or nullify an act of Congress, or absolve its citizens from their paramount obligation of obedience to the Constitution and laws of the United States.

Mr. Ewing moved to lay the same on the table; which was agreed to.

Mr. Field moved to amend the seventh section by striking out and inserting the following:

ARTICLE 1. No State shall withdraw from the Union without the consent of all the States, given in a Convention of the States, convened in pursuance of an act passed by two thirds of each House of Congress.

Mr. Clay raised a point of order as to this proposed amendment, and stated the point of order to be that the amendment was not germain to the subject-matter of the section.

The President over-ruled the point of order.

Mr. Goodrich moved to amend said amendment by inserting in lieu thereof the following:

"And no State can secede from the Union, or nullify an act of Congress, or absolve its citizens from their paramount obligations of obedience to the Constitution and laws of the United States."

The President decided the amendment not to be in order.

Mr. Field accepted certain amendments to his amendment, and moved to amend said section, by striking out and substituting the following, in lieu of section seven of said report:

"It is declared to be the true intent and meaning of the present Constitution, that the union of the States under it is indissoluble."

Mr. Buckner moved to amend the same by adding the following:

"But this declaration shall not be construed so as to give the Federal Government power or authority to coerce or to make war, directly or indirectly, upon a State, on account of a failure to comply with its obligations."

The question on agreeing to said amendment resulted in the following vote:

AYES—Delaware, Maryland, Missouri, North Carolina, Virginia—5.

NOES—Connecticut, Illinois, Indiana, Iowa, Maine, Massachusetts, New Jersey, New York, New Hampshire, Ohio, Pennsylvania, Rhode Island, Tennessee, Vermont, Kansas—15.

So the amendment was not agreed to.

Mr. Bronson moved to amend said amendment by striking out and inserting in lieu thereof the following:

" While we do not recognize the constitutional right of any State to secede from the Union, we are deeply impressed by the fact that this Government is not maintained by force, but by unity of origin and interest, inducing fraternal feelings between the people of different sections of the country, and our labors have been directed to the end of giving a new assurance to our brethren, North, South, East, and West, of our determination to stand firmly by all the compromises of the Constitution."

The question on the adoption of said amendment being called without a vote of States, the same was not agreed to.

The question recurring to the amendment of Mr. Field, was determined by the following vote:

AYES—Connecticut, Illinois, Indiana, Iowa, Maine, Massachusetts, New York, New Hampshire, Vermont, Kansas—10.

NOES—Delaware, Kentucky, Maryland, Missouri, New Jersey, North Carolina, Ohio, Pennsylvania, Rhode Island, Tennessee, Virginia—11.

So the amendment was not agreed to.

Mr. Somes moved to amend by adding the following as section 8.

" That the freedom of speech, or of the press, shall not be abridged ; but that the people of any Territory of the United States shall be left perfectly free to discuss the subject of slavery."

It was moved to lay the same on the table, and resulted in the following vote:

AYES—Delaware, Indiana, Kentucky, Maryland. Missouri, New Jersey, North Carolina, Ohio, Pennsylvania, Rhode Island, Tennessee, Virginia, Kansas—13.

NOES—Connecticut, Illinois, Iowa, Maine, Vermont—5.

So the amendment was laid on the table.

Mr. Vandever moved to amend the same by the following section:

" The navigation of the Mississippi river shall remain free to the people of each and all the States ; and Congress shall provide by law for the protection of commerce on said river against all interference, foreign or domestic.

It was moved to lay the same on the table, and resulted in the following vote:

AYES—Delaware, Indiana, Kentucky, Maryland, Missouri, New Jersey, North Carolina, New Hampshire, Ohio, Pennsylvania, Rhode Island, Tennessee, Vermont, Virginia—14.

NOES—Connecticut, Illinois, Iowa, Maine, Massachusetts, New York—6.

So the amendment was laid on the table.

Mr. Baldwin moved to strike out all the sections of the report, and insert the following:

Whereas, unhappy differences exist, which have alienated from each other portions of the people of the United States, to such an extent as seriously to disturb the peace of the nation and impair the regular and efficient action of the Government within the sphere of its constitutional powers and duties :

And, whereas, the Legislature of the State of Kentucky has made application to Congress to call a Convention for proposing amendments to the Constitution of the United States:

And whereas, it is believed to be the opinion of the people of other States that amendments to the Constitution are, or may become, necessary to secure to the people of the United States, of every section, the full and equal enjoyment of their rights and liberties, so far as the same may depend for their security and protection on the powers granted to, or withheld from the General Government, in pursuance of the national purposes for which it was ordained and established :

This Convention does, therefore, recommend to the several States to unite with Kentucky in her application to Congress to call a Convention for proposing amendments to the Constitution of the United States, to be submitted to the Legislatures of the several States, or to conventions therein, for ratification, as the one or the other mode of ratification may be proposed by Congress, in accordance with the provision in the fifth article of the Constitution.

The question on agreeing to said amendment resulted in the following vote:

Ayes—Connecticut, Illinois, Iowa, Maine, Massachusetts, New York, New Hampshire, Vermont—8.

Noes—Delaware, Indiana, Kentucky, Maryland, Missouri, New Jersey, North Carolina, Ohio, Pennsylvania, Rhode Island, Tennessee, Virginia, Kansas—13.

So the amendment was not agreed to.

The following gentlemen disagreed to the vote of their States:

Mr. Bronson, of New York.
Mr. Granger, of New York.
Mr. Dodge, of New York.
Mr. Corning, of New York.
Mr. Orth, of Indiana.
Mr. Hackleman, of Indiana.

Mr. Seddon, of Virginia, moved to amend said report by striking out and inserting as follows:

JOINT RESOLUTIONS proposing certain amendments to the Constitution of the United States.

Whereas, Serious and alarming dissensions have arisen between the northern and southern States, concerning the rights and security of the rights of the slaveholding States, and especially their rights in the common territory of the United States; and whereas, it is eminently desirable and proper that those dissensions, which now threaten the very existence of this Union, should be permanently quieted and settled by constitutional provisions, which shall do equal justice to all sections, and thereby restore to the people that peace and good will which ought to prevail between all the citizens of the United States; therefore,

Resolved by this Convention, that the following articles are hereby approved and submitted to the Congress of the United States, with the request that they may, by the requisite constitutional majority of two thirds, be recommended to the respective States of the Union, to be, when ratified by conventions of three fourths of the States, valid and operative as amendments of the Constitution of the Union.

Article 1. In all the territory of the United States now held or hereafter acquired, situate north of latitude thirty-six degrees and thirty minutes, slavery or involuntary servitude, except as a punishment for crime, is prohibited, while such territory shall remain under Territorial government. In all the territory now or hereafter acquired south of said line of latitude slavery of the African race is hereby recognized as existing, and shall not be interfered with by Congress; but shall be protected as property by all the departments of the Territorial government during its continuance; and when any Territory, north or south of said line, within such boundaries as Congress may prescribe, shall contain the population requisite for a member of Congress, according to the then federal ratio of representation of the people of the United States, it shall, if its form of government be republican, be admitted into the Union on an equal footing with the original States, with or without slavery, as the constitution of such new State may provide.

Article 2. Congress shall have no power to abolish slavery in places under its exclusive jurisdiction, and situate within the limits of States that permit the holding of slaves.

Article 3. Congress shall have no power to abolish slavery within the District of Columbia, so long as it exists in the adjoining States of Virginia and Maryland, or either, nor without the consent of the free white inhabitants, nor without just compensation first made to such owners of slaves as do not consent to such abolishment. Nor shall Congress at any time prohibit officers of the Federal Government or members of Congress, whose duties require them to be in said District, from bringing with them their slaves, and holding them as such, during the time their duties may require them to remain there, and afterwards taking them from the District.

Article 4. Congress shall have no power to prohibit or hinder the transportation of slaves from one State to another, or to a Territory in which slaves are by law permitted to be held, whether that transportation be by land, navigable rivers, or by the sea. And if such transportation be by sea, the slaves shall be protected as property by the Federal Government. And the right of transit by the owners with their slaves in passing to or from one slaveholding State or Territory to another, between and through the non-slaveholding States and Territories, shall be protected. And in imposing direct taxes pursuant to the Constitution, Congress shall have no power to impose on slaves a higher rate of tax than on land, according to their just value.

Article 5. That, in addition to the provisions of the third paragraph of the second section of the fourth article of the Constitution of the United States, Congress shall provide by law, that the United States shall pay to the owner who shall apply for it the full value of his fugitive slave in all cases when the marshal, or other officer, whose duty it was to arrest said fugitive, was prevented from so doing by violence or intimidation, or when, after arrest, said fugitive was res-

9

cued by force, and the owner thereby prevented and obstructed in the pursuit of his remo ly for the recovery of his fugitive slave, under the said clause of the Constitution and the laws made in pursuance thereof. And in all such cases, when the United States shall pay for such fugitive, they shall reimburse themselves by imposing and collecting a tax on the county or city in which said violence, intimidation, or rescue was committed, equal in amou t to the sum paid by them, with the addition of interest and the costs of collection; and the said county or city, after it has paid said amount to the United States, may, for its indemnity, sue and recover from the wrong-doers, or rescuers, by whom the owner was prevented from the recovery of his fugitive slave, in like manner as the owner himself might have sued and recovered.

ARTICLE 6. No future amendment of the Constitution shall affect the five preceding articles, nor the third paragraph of the second section of the first article of the Constitution, nor the third paragraph of the second section of the fourth article of said Constitution, and no amendment shall be made to the Constitution which will authorize or give to Congress any power to abolish or interfere with slavery in any of the States by whose laws it is or may be allowed or permitted.

ARTICLE 7. SEC. 1. The elective franchise and the right to hold office, whether Federal, State, Territorial, or municipal, shall not be exercised by persons who are, in whole or in part, of the African race.

And whereas, also, besides those causes of dissension embraced in the foregoing amendments proposed to the Constitution of the United States, there are others which come within the jurisdiction of Congress, and may be remedied by its legislative power; and whereas, it is the desire of this Convention, as far as its influence may extend, to remove all just cause for the popular discontent and agitation which now disturb the peace of the country, and threaten the stability of its institutions; therefore,

1. *Resolved*, That the laws now in force for the recovery of fugitive slaves are in strict pursuance of the plain and mandatory provisions of the Constitution, and have been sanctioned as valid and constitutional by the judgment of the Supreme Court of the United States; that the slaveholding States are entitled to the faithful observance and execution of those laws, and that they ought not to be repealed or so modified or changed as to impair their efficiency; and that laws ought to be made for the punishment of those who attempt, by rescue of the slave or other illegal means, to hinder or defeat the due execution of said laws.

2. That all State laws which conflict with the fugitive slave acts, or any other constitutional acts of Congress, or which in their operation impede, hinder, or delay the free course and due execution of any of said acts, are null and void by the plain provisions of the Constitution of the United States. Yet those State laws, void as they are, have given color to practices, and led to consequences which have obstructed the due administration and execution of acts of Congress, and especially the acts for the delivery of fugitive slaves, and have thereby contributed much to the discord and commotion now prevailing. This convention, therefore, in the present perilous juncture, does not deem it improper, respectfully and earnestly, to recommend the repeal of those laws to the several States which have enacted them, or such legislative corrections or explanations of them as may prevent their being used or perverted to such mischievous purposes.

3. That the act of the eighteenth of September, eighteen hundred and fifty, commonly called the fugitive slave law, ought to be so amended as to make the fee of the commissioner, mentioned in the eighth section of the act, equal in amount, in the cases decided by him, whether his decision be in favor of or against the claimant. And to avoid misconstruction, the last clause of the fifth section of said act, which authorizes the person holding a warrant for the arrest or detention of a fugitive slave to summon to his aid the posse comitatus, and which declares it to be the duty of all good citizens to assist him in its execution, ought to be so amended as to expressly limit the authority and duty to cases in which there shall be resistance, or danger of resistance or rescue.

4. That the laws for the suppression of the African slave trade, and especially those prohibiting the importati n of slaves into the United States, ought to be made effectual, and ought to be thoroughly executed, and all further enactments necessary to those ends ought to be promptly made.

The question on agreeing to said amendment resulted in the following vote:

AYES—Kentucky, Missouri, North Carolina, Virginia—4.

NOES—Connecticut, Delaware, Illinois, Indiana, Maine, Massachusetts, Maryland, New Jersey, New York, New Hampshire, Ohio, Pennsylvania, Rhode Island, Tennessee, Vermont, Kansas—16.

So the amendment was not agreed to.

Mr. Dent, of Maryland, dissented from the vote of his State.

Mr. Clay, according to previous notice, moved to amend said report by striking out the same, and inserting the following:

WHEREAS the Union is in danger; and owing to the unhappy divisions existing in Congress, it would be difficult, if not impossible, for that body to concur, in both its branches, by the requisite majority, so as to enable it either to adopt such measures of legislation, or to recommend to the States such amendments to the Constitution as are deemed necessary and proper to avert that danger; and whereas in so great an emergency, the opinion and judgment of the people ought to be heard, and would be the best and surest guide to their representatives; therefore,

Resolved, That provision ought to be made by law, without delay, for taking the sense of the people, and submitting to their vote the following resolutions as the basis for the final and permanent settlement of those disputes that now disturb the peace of the country and threaten the existence of the Union.

And that whereas, serious and alarming dissensions have arisen between the Northern and Southern States, concerning the rights and security of the rights of the slaveholding States, and especially their rights in the common territory of the United States; and whereas, it is eminently desirable and proper that those dissensions, which now threaten the very existence of this Union, should be permanently quieted and settled by constitutional provisions, which shall do equal justice to all sections, and thereby restore to the people that peace and good will which ought to prevail between all the citizens of the United States : therefore,

Resolved, That the following articles be, and are hereby, proposed and submitted as amendments to the Constitution of the United States, which shall be valid to all intents and purposes as part of said Constitution, when ratified by conventions of three fourths of the several States.

ARTICLE 1. In all the territory of the United States now held, or hereafter acquired, situate north of latitude thirty-six degrees and thirty minutes, slavery or involuntary servitude, except as a punishment for crime, is prohibited, while such territory shall remain under territorial government. In all the territory south of said line of latitude slavery of the African race is hereby recognized as existing, and shall not be interfered with by Congress ; but shall be protected as property by all the departments of the territorial government during its continuance ; and when any territory north or south of said line, within such boundaries as Congress may prescribe, shall contain the population requisite for a member of Congress, according to the then federal ratio of representation of the people of the United States, it shall, if its form of government be republican, be admitted into the Union on an equal footing with the original States, with or without slavery, as the constitution of such new State may provide.

ARTICLE 2. Congress shall have no power to abolish slavery in places under its exclusive jurisdiction, and situate within the limits of States that permit the holding of slaves.

ARTICLE 3. Congress shall have no power to abolish slavery within the District of Columbia, so long as it exists in the adjoining States of Virginia and Maryland, or either, nor without the consent of the inhabitants, nor without just compensation first made to such owners of slaves as do not consent to such abolishment. Nor shall Congress at any time prohibit officers of the Federal Government, or members of Congress, whose duties require them to be in said District, from bringing with them their slaves, and holding them as such during the time their duties may require them to remain there, and afterwards taking them from the District.

ARTICLE 4. Congress shall have no power to prohibit or hinder the transportation of slaves from one State to another, or to a Territory in which slaves are by law permitted to be held, whether that transportation be by land, navigable rivers, or by the sea. And the right of transit by the owners with their slaves, in passing to or from one slaveholding State or Territory to another, between and through the non-slaveholding States and Territories, shall be protected.

ARTICLE 5. That, in addition to the provisions of the third paragraph of the second section of the fourth article of the Constitution of the United States, Congress shall have power to provide by law, and it shall be its duty so to provide, that the United States shall pay to the owner who shall apply for it, the full value of his fugitive slave, in all cases, when the marshal, or other officer, whose duty it was to arrest said fugitive, was prevented from so doing by violence or intimidation, or when, after arrest, said fugitive was rescued by force, and the owner thereby prevented and obstructed in the pursuit of his remedy for the recovery of his fugitive slave, under the said clause of the Constitution and the laws made in pursuance thereof. And in all such cases, when the United States shall pay for such fugitive, they shall have the power to reimburse themselves by imposing and collecting a tax on the county or city in which said violence, intimidation, or rescue was committed, equal in amount to the sum paid by them, with the addition of interest and the costs of collection; and the said county or city after it has paid said amount to the United States, may, for its indemnity, sue and recover from the wrong-doers, or rescuers, by whom the owner was prevented from the recovery of his fugitive slave, in like manner as the owner himself might have sued and recovered

ARTICLE 6. No future amendment of the Constitution shall affect the five preceding articles, nor the third paragraph of the second section of the first article of the Constitution, nor the third paragraph of the second section of the fourth article of said Constitution, and no amendment shall be made to the Constitution which will authorize or give to Congress any power to abolish or interfere with slavery in any of the States by whose laws it is or may be allowed or permitted.

ARTICLE 7. Sec. 1. The elective franchise and the right to hold office, whether federal, State, territorial, or municipal, shall not be exercised by persons who are, in whole or in part, of the African race.

SEC. 2. The United States shall have power to acquire from time to time, districts of country, in Africa and South America, for the colonization, at expense of the federal Treasury, of such free negroes and mulattoes as the several States may wish to have removed from their limits, and from the District of Columbia, and such other places as may be under the jurisdiction of Congress.

And whereas, also, besides those causes of dissension embraced in the foregoing amendments proposed to the Constitution of the United States, there are others which come within the jurisdiction of Congress, and may be remedied by its legislative power; and whereas, it is the desire of this Convention, as far as its influence may extend, to remove all just cause for the popular discontent and agitation which now disturb the peace of the country, and threaten the stability of its institutions: therefore,

1. *Resolved*, That the laws now in force for the recovery of fugitive slaves are in strict pursuance of the plain and mandatory provisions of the Constitution, and have been sanctioned as valid and constitutional by the judgment of the Supreme Court of the United States; that the slaveholding States are entitled to the faithful observance and execution of those laws, and that they ought not to be repealed or so modified or changed as to impair their efficiency; and that laws ought to be made for the punishment of those who attempt, by rescue of the slave or other illegal means, to hinder or defeat the due execution of said laws.

2. That all State laws which conflict with the fugitive slave acts, or any other constitutional acts of Congress, or which in their operation impede, hinder, or delay the free course and due execution of any of said acts, are null and void by the plain provisions of the Constitution of the United States. Yet those State laws, void as they are, have given color to practices, and led to consequences which have obstructed the due administration and execution of acts of Congress, and especially the acts for the delivery of fugitive slaves, and have thereby contributed much to the discord and commotion now prevailing. This Convention, therefore, in the present perilous juncture, does not deem it improper, respectfully and earnestly, to recommend the repeal of those laws to the several States which have enacted them, or such legislative corrections or explanations of them as may prevent their being used or perverted to such mischievous purposes.

3. That the act of the eighteenth of September, eighteen hundred and fifty, commonly called the fugitive slave law, ought to be so amended as to make the fee of the commissioner, mentioned in the eighth section of the act, equal in amount, in the cases decided by him, whether his decision be in favor of or against the claimant. And to avoid misconstruction, the last clause of the fifth section of said act, which authorizes the person holding a warrant for the arrest or detention of a fugitive slave to summon to his aid the posse comitatus, and which declares it to be the duty of all good citizens to assist him in its execution, ought to be so amended as to expressly limit the authority and duty to cases in which there shall be resistance, or danger of resistance or rescue.

4. That the laws for the suppression of the African slave trade, and especially those prohibiting the importation of slaves into the United States, ought to be made effectual, and ought to be thoroughly executed, and all further enactments necessary to those ends ought to be promptly made.

The question on agreeing to said amendment resulted in the following vote:

AYES—Kentucky, Missouri, North Carolina, Tennessee, Virginia—5.

NOES—Connecticut, Delaware, Illinois, Indiana, Maine, Massachusetts, Maryland, New Jersy, New York, New Hampshire, Ohio, Pennsylvania, Rhode Island, Vermont—14.

So the amendment was not agreed to.

Mr. Dent, of Maryland, dissented from the vote of his State.

Mr. Tuck, of New Hampshire, moved to amend said report by striking out, and inserting as follows:

TO THE PEOPLE OF THE UNITED STATES:

On the 4th day of February, 1861, in compliance with the invitation of the State of Virginia, commissioners from several other States met the commissioners of that State in Conference Convention, in the city of Washington. From time to time, commissioners from other States appeared, appointed, as were those who first appeared, some by the Legislatures, and some by the Governors of their respective States, until, on the 23d instant, twenty-one States were then represented. The Convention thus constituted claims no authority under the Constitution and laws; but deeply impressed with a sense of existing dissensions and dangers, proceeded to a careful consideration of them and their appropriate remedies, and having brought their deliberations to a close, now submit the result to the judgment of their fellow-citizens.

We recognize and deplore the divisions and distractions which now afflict our country, interrupt its prosperity, disturb its peace, and endanger the Union of the States; but we repel the conclusion that any alienations or dissensions exist which are irreconcilable, which justify attempts at revolution, or which the patriotism and fraternal sentiments of the people, and the interests and honor of the whole nation, will not overcome.

In a country embracing the central and most important portion of a continent, among a people now numbering over thirty millions, diversities of opinion inevitably exist; and rivalries, intensified at times by local interests and sectional attachments, must often occur; yet we do not doubt that the theory of our government is the best which is possible for this nation, that the Union of the States is of vital importance, and that the Constitution, which expresses the combined wisdom of the illustrious founders of the government, is still the palladium of our liberties, adequate to every emergency, and justly entitled to the support of every good citizen.

It embraces, in its provisions and spirit, all the defense and protection which any section of the country can rightfully demand, or honorably concede.

Adopted with primary reference to the wants of five millions of people, but with the wisest reference to future expansion and development, it has carried us onward with a rapid increase of numbers, an accumulation of wealth, and a degree of happiness and general prosperity never attained by any other nation.

Whatever branch of industry, or whatever staple production shall become, in the possible changes of the future, the leading interest of the country, thereby creating unforeseen complications or new conflicts of opinion and interest, the Constitution of the United States, properly understood, and fairly enforced, is equal to every exigency, a shield and defense to all in every time of need. If, however, by reason of a change in circumstances, or for any cause, a portion of the people believe they ought to have their rights more exactly defined or more fully explained in the Constitution, it is their duty, in accordance with its provisions, to seek a remedy by way of amendment to that instrument; and it is the duty of all the States to concur in such amendments as may be found necessary to insure equal and exact justice to all.

In order, therefore, to announce to the country the sentiments of this Convention, respecting not only the remedy which should be sought for existing discontents, but also to communicate to the public what we believe to be the patriotic sentiment of the country, we adopt the following resolutions:

1st. *Resolved,* That this Convention recognize the well understood proposition that the Constitution of the United States gives no power to Congress, or any branch of the Federal Government to interfere in any manner with slavery in any of the States; and we are assured, by abundant testimony, that neither of the great political organizations existing in the country contemplates a violation of the spirit of the Constitution in this regard, or the procuring of any amendment thereof, by which Congress, or any department of the General Government, shall ever have jurisdiction over slavery in any of the States.

2d *Resolved,* That the Constitution was ordained and established, as set forth in the preamble, by the people of the United States, in order to form a more perfect Union, establish justice, insure domestic tranquility, provide for the common defense, promote the general welfare, and secure the blessings of liberty to themselves and their posterity; and when the people of any State are not in full enjoyment of all the benefits intended to be secured to them by the Constitution, or their rights under it are disregarded, their tranquility disturbed, their prosperity retarded, or their liberty imperiled by the people of any other State, full and adequate redress can and ought to be provided for such grievances.

3d. *Resolved,* That the Constitution of the United States, and the acts of Congress in pursuance thereof, are the supreme law of the land, to which every citizen owes faithful obedience; and it is therefore respectfully recommended to the Legislatures of the several States to consider impartially whatever complaints may be made of acts, as inconsistent therewith, by sister States or their citizens, and carefully revise their statutes, in view of such complaints, and to repeal whatever provisions may be found to be in contravention of that supreme law.

4th. *Resolved,* That this Convention recommend to the Legislatures of the several States of the Union to follow the example of the Legislatures of the States of Kentucky and of Illinois, in applying to Congress to call a Convention for the proposing of amendments to the Constitution of the United States, pursuant to the fifth article thereof.

The question on agreeing to said amendment resulted in the following vote:

Ayes—Connecticut, Illinois, Indiana, Iowa, Maine, Massachusetts, New York, New Hampshire, Vermont—9.

Noes—Delaware, Kentucky, Maryland, Missouri, New Jersey, North Carolina, Ohio, Pennsylvania, Rhode Island, Tennessee, Virginia—11.

So the amendment was not agreed to.

Mr. Brockenbrough proposed to amend said report by what he read.

The Chair ruled the same out of order.

Mr. Guthrie moved that the Convention proceed to vote on the sections of the report as amended, section by section; which was agreed to.

Mr. Ellis, of Indiana, moved so to amend the rule that the report shall be taken up, and each section and each distinct proposition be voted on separately.

The Chair determined the motion was out of order.

Mr. Guthrie moved the adoption of the 1st section, as follows:

ARTICLE 13.

SECTION 1. In all the present territory of the United States, north of the parallel of thirty-six degrees and thirty minutes of north latitude, involuntary servitude, except in punishment of crime, is prohibited. In all the present territory south of that line, the status of persons held to involuntary service or labor, as it now exists, shall not be changed ; nor shall any law be passed by Congress or the Territorial Legislature to hinder or prevent the taking of such persons from any of the States of this Union to said territory, nor to impair the rights arising from said relation; but the same shall be subject to judicial cognizance in the federal courts, according to the course of the common law. When any territory north or south of said line, within such boundary as Congress may prescribe, shall contain a population equal to that required for a member of Congress, it shall, if its form of government be republican, be admitted into the Union on an equal footing with the original States, with or without involuntary servitude, as the constitution of such State may provide.

The question on agreeing to said section resulted in the following vote:

AYES—Delaware, Kentucky, Maryland, New Jersey, Ohio, Pennsylvania, Rhode Island, Tennessee—8.

NOES—Connecticut, Illinois, Iowa, Maine, Massachusetts, Missouri, New York, North Carolina, New Hampshire, Vermont, Virginia—11.

So the section was not agreed to.

The following gentlemen dissented from the vote of their States:

Mr. Ruffin and Mr. Morehead, of North Carolina.

Mr. Totten, of Tennessee.

Mr. Coalter and Mr. Hough, of Missouri.

Mr. Bronson, Mr. Corning, Mr. Dodge, Mr. Wool, and Mr. Granger, of New York.

Mr. Meredith and Mr. Wilmot, of Pennsylvania.

Mr. Rives and Mr. Summers of Virginia.

Mr. Clay and Mr. Butler, of Kentucky.

Mr. Logan, of Illinois.

A reconsideration of said vote was called by Illinois, and agreed to—14 to 5.

Pending the consideration of said section, Mr. Granger moved an adjournment to half-past 7 o'clock, P. M.

The Convention then adjourned.

7½ O'CLOCK, P. M.

The Convention assembled according to adjournment.

Mr. Wickliffe, of Kentucky, moved the Convention adjourn to 10 o'clock, the 27th.

Which was agreed to—ayes 17, noes 5.

So the Convention adjourned.

WASHINGTON CITY, *February* 27, 1861.

The Convention met pursuant to adjournment.

President Tyler in the chair.

The proceedings were opened with prayer from the Rev. Dr. Gurley.

The order of the day was the adoption of the first section.

Mr. Guthrie moved the adoption of the first section of the report, as amended, and reading as follows:

SECTION 1. In all the present territory of the United States, north of the parallel of thirty-six degrees and thirty minutes of north latitude, involuntary servitude, except in punishment of crime, is prohibited. In all the present territory south of that line, the status of persons held to involuntary service or labor, as it now exists, shall not be changed; nor shall any law be passed by Congress or the Territorial Legislature to hinder or prevent the taking of such persons from any of the States of this Union to said territory, nor to impair the rights arising from said relation; but the same shall be subject to judicial cognizance in the federal courts, according to the course of the common law. When any territory north or south of said line, within such boundary as Congress may prescribe, shall contain a population equal to that required for a member of Congress, it shall, if its form of government be republican, be admitted into the Union on an equal footing with the original States, with or without involuntary servitude, as the constitution of such State may provide.

The question on the adoption of said section resulted in the following vote:

AYES—Delaware, Illinois, Kentucky, Maryland, New Jersey, Ohio, Pennsylvania, Rhode Island, Tennessee—9.

NOES—Connecticut, Iowa, Maine, Massachusetts, North Carolina, New Hampshire, Vermont, Virginia—8.

So the section was adopted.

On calling New York, the members stated that one of their number was absent, and the delegation were divided. Inquiry was made of the President whether an absent member could vote. The President decided he could not, without general leave.

New York, Indiana, and Kansas were divided.

When Indiana was called to vote on the first section, Mr. Hackelman rose and said:

The Commissioners of Indiana were appointed by virtue of resolutions passed by the Legislature of that State, which required them to report to the Legislature any proposition before voting for it finally, so as to commit the State. It is impossible to obtain the time to submit the proposed amendments to the Legislature of Indiana for its approval or rejection. Indiana, therefore, declines to vote.

Indiana having declined to vote, Mr. T. C. Slaughter asked to have his individual vote entered in the affirmative on first section.

Mr. Ellis, of Indiana, for the reason stated above, asked to have his individual vote entered in the negative on the first section.

The following gentlemen dissented from the vote of their States:

Mr. Clay and Mr. Butler, of Kentucky.

Mr. Ruffin and Mr. Morehead, of North Carolina.

Mr. Meredith and Mr. Wilmot, of Pennsylvania.

Mr. Totten, of Tennessee.

Mr. Cook, of Illinois.

Mr. Rives and Mr. Summers, of Virginia.

Mr. Chase and Mr. Wolcott, of Ohio.

Mr. Guthrie moved the adoption of the second section of the report, as amended, and reading as follows:

SECTION 2. No territory shall be acquired by the United States, except by discovery, and for naval and commercial stations, depots, and transit routes, without the concurrence of a majority of all the Senators from States which allow involuntary servitude, and a majority of all the Senators from States which prohibit that relation; nor shall territory be acquired by treaty, unless the votes of a majority of the Senators from each class of States hereinbefore mentioned be cast as a part of the two thirds majority necessary to the ratification of such treaty.

The question on the adoption of said section resulted in the following vote:

AYES—Delaware, Indiana, Kentucky, Maryland, Missouri, New Jersey, Ohio, Pennsylvania, Rhode Island, Tennessee. Virginia—11.

NOES—Connecticut, Illinois, Iowa, Maine, Massachusetts, North Carolina, New Hampshire, Vermont—8.

New York and Kansas were divided.

So the section was adopted.

The following gentlemen dissented from the vote of their States:

> Mr. Meredith and Mr. Wilmot, of Pennsylvania.
> Mr. Ruffin and Mr. Morehead, of North Carolina.
> Mr. Tyler, of Virginia.
> Mr. Clay, of Kentucky.
> Mr. Hackelman and Mr. Orth, of Indiana.

Mr. Guthrie, of Kentucky, moved the adoption of the third section of the report, as amended, and reading as follows:

SECTION 3. Neither the Constitution, nor any amendment thereof, shall be construed to give Congress power to regulate, abolish, or control, with n any St te, the relation established or recognized by the laws thereof touching persons held to labor or involuntary service therein, nor to interfere with or abolish involuntary service in the District of Columbia without the consent of Maryland and without the consent of the owners, or making the owners who do not consent just compensation; nor the power to interfere with or prohibit Representatives and others from bringing with them to the District of Columbia, retaining, and taking away, persons so held to labor or service; nor the power to interfere with or abolish involuntary service in places under the exclusive jurisdiction of the United States within those States and Territories where the same is established or recognized; nor the power to prohibit the removal or transportation of persons held to labor or involuntary service in any State or Territory of the United States to any other State or Territory thereof where it is established or recognized by law or usage; and the right durin g transportation, by sea or river, of touching at ports, shores, and landings, and of landing in case of distress, shall exist; but not the right of transit in or through any State or Territory, or of sale or traffic, against the laws thereof. Nor shall Congress have power to authorize any higher rate of taxation on persons held to labor or service than on land.

The bringing into the District of Columbia of persons held to labor or service for sale, or placing them in depots to be afterwards transferred to other places for sale as merchandise, is prohibited.

The question on the adoption of said section resulted in the following vote:

AYES—Delaware, Illinois. Kentucky, Maryland, Missouri, New Jersey, North Carolina, Ohio, Pennsylvania, Rhode Island, Tennessee, Virginia—12.

NOES—Connecticut, Indiana, Iowa, Maine, Massachusetts, New Hampshire, Vermont—7.

New York and Kansas were divided.

So the section was adopted.

The following gentlemen dissented from the vote of their States:

> Mr. Clay, of Kentucky.
> Mr. Cook, of Illinois.
> Mr. Slaughter, of Indiana.
> Mr. Chase and Mr. Wolcott, of Ohio.

Mr. Guthrie, of Kentucky, moved the adoption of the fourth section of the report, as amended, and reading as follows:

SECTION 4. The third paragraph of the second section of the fourth article of the Constitution shall not be construed to prevent any of the States, by appropriate legislation, and through the action of their judicial and ministerial officers, from enforcing the delivery of fugitives from labor to the person to whom such service or labor is due.

The question on the adoption of said section resulted in the following vote:

AYES—Connecticut, Delaware, Illinois, Indiana, Kentucky, Maryland, Missouri, New Jersey, North Carolina, Ohio, Pennsylvania, Rhode Island, Tennessee, Vermont, Virginia—15.

NOES—Iowa, Maine, Massachusetts, New Hampshire—4.

New York and Kansas were divided.

So the section was adopted.

The following gentlemen dissented from the vote of their States:

> Mr. Baldwin, of Connecticut.
> Mr. Hackleman, Mr. Orth, of Indiana.
> Mr. Chase, Mr. Wolcott, of Ohio.

Mr. Guthrie, of Kentucky, moved the adoption of the fifth section of the report, as amended, and reading as follows:

SECTION 5. The foreign slave trade is hereby forever prohibited; and it shall be the duty of Congress to pass laws to prevent the importation of slaves, coolies, or persons held to service or labor, into the United States and the Territories from places beyond the limits thereof.

The question on the adoption of said section resulted in the following vote:

AYES—Connecticut, Delaware, Illinois, Indiana, Kentucky, Maryland, Missouri, New Jersey, New York, New Hampshire, Ohio, Pennsylvania, Rhode Island, Tennessee, Vermont, and Kansas—16.

NOES—Iowa, Maine, Massachusetts, North Carolina, and Virginia—5.

So this section was adopted.

The following gentlemen dissented from the vote of their States:

Mr. Baldwin, of Connecticut.
Mr. Clay, of Kentucky.
Mr. Ruffin, Mr. Morehead, of North Carolina.
Mr. Wolcott, Mr. Chase, of Ohio.
Mr. Hackleman, Mr. Orth, of Indiana.

Mr. Guthrie, of Kentucky, moved the adoption of the sixth section of the report as amended, and reading as follows:

SECTION 6. The first, third, and fifth sections, together with this section of these amendments, and the third paragraph of the second section of the first article of the Constitution, and the third paragraph of the second section of the fourth article thereof, shall not be amended or abolished without the consent of all the States.

The question on the adoption of said section resulted in the following vote:

AYES—Delaware, Illinois, Kentucky, Maryland, Missouri, New Jersey, Ohio, Pennsylvania, Rhode Island, Tennessee, Kansas—11.

NOES—Connecticut, Indiana, Iowa, Maine, Massachusetts, North Carolina, New Hampshire, Vermont, Virginia—9.

New York was divided.

So this section was adopted.

The following gentlemen dissented from the vote of their States:

Mr. Ruffin, Mr. Morehead, of North Carolina.
Mr. Wolcott, Mr. Chase, of Ohio.
Mr. Cook, of Illinois.
Mr. Summers, Mr. Rives, of Virginia.

Mr. Guthrie, of Kentucky, moved the adoption of the seventh section of the report, as amended, and reading as follows:

SECTION 7. Congress shall provide by law that the United States shall pay to the owner the full value of his fugitive from labor, in all cases where the marshal, or other officer, whose duty it was to arrest such fugitive, was prevented from so doing by violence or intimidation from mobs or riotous assemblages, or when, after arrest, such fugitive was rescued by like violence or intimidation, and the owner thereby deprived of the same; and the acceptance of such payment shall preclude the owner from further claim to such fugitive. Congress shall provide by law for securing to the citizens of each State the privileges and immunities of citizens in the several States.

The question on the adoption of said section resulted in the following vote:

AYES—Delaware Illinois, Indiana, Kentucky, Maryland, New Jersey, New Hampshire, Ohio, Pennsylvania, Rhode Island, Tennessee, Kansas—12.

NOES—Connecticut, Iowa, Maine, Missouri, North Carolina, Vermont, Virginia—7.

New York was divided.

So this last section was adopted.

10

The following gentlemen dissented from the vote of their States:

Mr. Ruffin, of North Carolina.
Mr. Morehead, of North Carolina.
Mr. Totten, of Tennessee.
Mr. Hackleman, of Indiana.
Mr. Orth, of Indiana.
Mr. Chase, of Ohio.
Mr. Wolcott, of Ohio.

Mr. Chase called for the consideration of the seven propositions as a whole collectively.

The President decided that the Convention, having gone through, amended, and adopted said sections in severalty, and then having determined and passed on the same as amended in severalty, the whole were adopted, and no further vote could be taken.

Mr. Chase appealed from the decision of the President.

The President stated his decision.

Mr. Chase withdrew his appeal.

Mr. Franklin, of Pennsylvania, moved the adoption of the following resolution:

Resolved, As the sense of this Convention, that the highest political duty of every citizen of the United States is his allegiance to the Federal Government, created by the Constitution of the United States, and that no State of this Union has any constitutional right to secede therefrom, or to absolve the citizens of such State from their allegiance to the Government of the United States.

Mr. Barringer moved to lay the resolution on the table. And the vote by States resulted as follows:

AYES—Delaware, Kentucky, Maryland, Missouri, New Jersey, North Carolina, Ohio, Tennessee, Virginia—9.

NOES—Connecticut, Illinois, Indiana, Iowa, Maine, Massachusetts, New York, New Hampshire, Pennsylvania, Rhode Island, Vermont, Kansas—12.

The Convention refused to lay on the table.

Mr. Coalter, of Missouri, offered the following as an amendment and substitute:

The term of office of all Presidents and Vice Presidents of the United States hereafter elected shall be six years; and any person once elected to either of said offices shall ever after be ineligible to the same office.

Which was laid on the table.

Mr. Seddon moved to amend by striking out and inserting his second act of amendments, as follows:

To secure concert and promote harmony between the slaveholding and non-slaveholding sections of the Union, the assent of the majority of the Senators from the slaveholding States, and of the majority of the Senators from the non-slaveholding States, shall be requisite to the validity of all action of the Senate, on which the ayes and noes may be called by five Senators.

And on a written declaration, signed and presented for record on the journal of the Senate by a majority of the Senators from either the non-slaveholding or slaveholding States, of their want of confidence in any officer or appointee of the Executive, exercising functions exclusively or continuously within the class of States, or any of them, which the signers represent, then such officer shall be removed by the Executive; and if not removed at the expiration of ten days from the presentation of such declaration, the office shall be deemed vacant, and open to new appointment.

The connection of every State with the Union is recognized as depending on the continuing assent of its people, and compulsion shall in no case, nor under any form, be attempted by the government of the Union against a State acting in its collective or organic capacity. Any State, by the action of a convention of its people, assembled pursuant to a law of its Legislature, is held entitled to dissolve its relation to the Federal Government, and withdraw from the Union; and, on due notice given of such withdrawal to the Executive of the Union, he shall appoint two commissioners, to meet two commissioners to be appointed by the Governor of the State, who, with the aid, if needed from the disagreement of the commissioners, of an umpire, to be selected by a majority of them, shall equitably adjudicate and determine finally a partition of the rights and obligations of the withdrawing State; and such adjudication and partition being accomplished, the withdrawal of such State shall be recognized by the Executive, and announced by public proclamation to the world.

But such withdrawing State shall not afterwards be re-admitted into the Union without the assent of two thirds of the States constituting the Union at the time of the proposed re-admission.

The amendments were laid on the table, with leave to have them placed on the journal.

The question recurring to the amendment proposed by Mr. Franklin,

Mr. Ruffin moved to postpone the consideration of the same indefinitely; and the same was postponed, by the following vote:

AYES—Delaware, Kentucky, Maryland, Missouri, New Jersey, North Carolina, Ohio, Rhode Island, Tennessee, Virginia—10.

NOES—Connecticut, Illinois, Indiana, Iowa, Maine, Massachusetts, Pennsylvania—7.

New York was divided.

Mr. Duncan, of Rhode Island, dissented from the vote of his State.

Mr. Ames dissented from his State.

Mr. Guthrie offered the following preamble.

To THE CONGRESS OF THE UNITED STATES:

The Convention assembled upon the invitation of the State of Virginia to adjust the unhappy differences which now disturb the peace of the Union and threaten its continuance, make known to the Congress of the United States that their body convened in the city of Washington on the 4th instant, and continued in session until the 27th.

There were in the body, when action was taken upon that which is here submitted, one hundred and thirty-three commissioners, representing the following States: Maine, New Hampshire, Vermont, Massachusetts, Rhode Island, Connecticut, New York, New Jersey, Pennsylvania, Delaware, Maryland, Virginia, North Carolina, Tennessee, Kentucky, Missouri, Ohio, Indiana, Illinois, Iowa, Kansas.

They have approved what is herewith submitted, and respectfully request that your honorable body will submit it to conventions in the States as an article of amendment to the Constitution of the United States.

Mr. Randolph moved that the preamble be adopted, and that the same, together with the seven propositions, be authenticated by the President and Secretary, and the same should be presented by President Tyler to the Senate and House of Representatives, and ask the passage thereof.

Agreed to.

Mr. Barringer moved that the injunction of secrecy against speaking of the action of the Convention, or the publication of its proceedings, be now removed.

Agreed to.

Mr. Johnson, of Missouri, asked leave to offer and have placed in this journal, the following:

Resolved, That while the adoption, by the States of South Carolina, Georgia, Florida, Alabama, Mississippi, Louisiana, and Texas, of ordinances declaring the dissolution of their relations with the Union, is an event deeply to be deplored, and while abstaining from any judgment on their conduct, we would express the earnest hope that they may soon see cause to resume their honored places in this confederacy of States; yet to the end that such return may be facilitated, and from the conviction that the Union being formed by the assent of the people of the respective States, and being compatible only with freedom, and the republican institutions guarantied to each, cannot and ought not to be maintained by force, we deprecate any effort by the federal Government to coerce, in any form, the said States to re-union or submission, as tending to irreparable breach, and leading to incalculable ills; and we earnestly invoke the abstinence from all counsels or measures of compulsion towards them.

Leave was granted.

Mr. Pollock, on behalf of the Committee on Finance, reported that they had examined into the expenses necessary to be met by the Convention. That the printing of the journal would be done by the city. They have found that the aggregate amount will be $735. The portion of each State is consequently $35, if the Convention decide to make an equal instalment upon all the States.

Mr. Brown moved the adoption of the following:

Resolved, That the report of the committee be received and accepted; that the committee be continued, and requested to make the necessary disbursements; and that the States now pay over the sum assessed to the chairman.

Which was agreed to.

Mr. Loomis, of Pennsylvania, sent to the Secretary's table and caused to be read the following letter:

CRAFTS J. WRIGHT, Esq.,
    Secretary Conference Convention :

SIR : Please inform the Convention that we have tendered, free of charge, the use of our hall and lights, which they have occupied. We hope the use may be sanctified by restoring peace to the Union.   We are, respectfully, &c.,
    FEBRUARY 23, 1861.   J. C. & H. A. WILLARD.

Whereupon Mr. Loomis offered and asked the adoption of the following resolution :

Resolved, That the thanks of this Convention are justly due, and are hereby given, to the Messrs. Willard for the liberal and generous tender, free of charge, of the use of the hall and the lights for the purposes expressed in their letter to the Secretary ; and that the Secretary be requested to communicate to them a copy of this resolution.

Which was unanimously agreed to.

Mr. Dodge, of New York, moved the adoption of the following:

Resolved, That the thanks of this Convention are justly due, and are hereby given, to the Mayor and Council of the city of Washington, for their kindness and liberality to the members of this Convention, in defraying so large an amount of their expenses for printing and stationery, and also for the officers to protect this hall and the members from intrusion whilst in session, and that the Secretary be requested to communicate the same to said parties.

Which was unanimously agreed to.

Mr. Randolph moved that the thanks of the Convention are justly due and be given to the clergy of the city, for their kind services during the Convention; which was unanimously agreed to.

The thanks of the Convention were presented to the Secretary and his assistants.

Mr. Ewing, of Ohio, moved the adoption of the following :

Resolved, That the thanks of this Convention be tendered to the President for the dignified and impartial manner in which he has presided over the deliberations of this body.

Which was unanimously agreed to: whereupon President Tyler returned to the Convention appropriate thanks.

Mr. Wickliffe, of Kentucky, moved that the Convention now close its session and adjourn ; that they informally meet and take parting leave of each other at 3 o'clock.

Mr. Brown moved to amend the same by now adjourning without day; which was carried by the following vote:

AYES—Delaware, Illinois, Kentucky, Maryland, New Jersey, Ohio, Rhode Island, Tennessee, Vermont—9.
NOES—Connecticut, Indiana, Missouri, North Carolina, Pennsylvania—6.

So the Convention adjourned without day.

NOTE.—The proposition of Judge Brockenbrough which was to be placed on the journal, has not been sent to the Secretary by Judge B.

WASHINGTON CITY, *March 9th*, 1861.

The undersigned hereby certifies that the foregoing Journal, printed by McGill & Witherow, has been printed from the original manuscript Journal of the Conference Convention, which began its session in this city February 4th, and terminated February 27th, 1861, and that the said printed copy has been carefully compared with the original papers, and found to be accurate. CRAFTS J. WRIGHT,

Secretary.

DELEGATES TO THE CONFERENCE CONVENTION.

MAINE.

William P. Fessenden,	Biddeford.
Lot M. Morrell,	
Daniel E. Somes,	Biddeford.
John J. Perry,	Oxford.
Ezra B. French,	Damaris Cotta.
Freeman H. Morse,	Bath.
Stephen Coburn,	
Stephen C. Foster,	Pembroke.

NEW HAMPSHIRE.

Amos Tuck,	Exeter.
Levi Chamberlain,	
Asa Fowler,	Concord,

VERMONT.

Hiland Hall,	North Bennington.
Levi Underwood,	Burlington.
H. Henry Baxter,	Rutland.
L. E. Chittenden,	Burlington.
B. D. Harris,	Brattleboro'.

MASSACHUSETTS.

John Z. Goodrich,	Stockbridge.
Charles Allen,	Worcester.
George S. Boutwell,	Boston.
Theophilus P. Chandler,	Boston.
Francis B. Crowninshield,	Boston.
John M. Forbes,	Boston.
Richard P. Waters,	Salem.

RHODE ISLAND.

Samuel Ames,	- - - - -	Providence.
Alexander Duncan,	- - - - -	Providence.
William W. Hoppin,	- - - -	Providence.
George H. Brown,	- - - -	Providence.
Samuel G. Arnold, -	- - - -	Providence.

CONNECTICUT.

Roger S. Baldwin,	- - - -	Weindham.
Chauncey F. Cleveland,	- - - -	
Charles J. McCurdy,	- - - -	Lyme.
James T. Pratt,	- - - - -	
Robins Battell, -	- - - -	
Amos S. Treat,	- - - -	Bridgeport.

NEW YORK.

David Dudley Field,	- - - -	New York.
William Curtis Noyes,	- - - -	New York.
James S. Wadsworth,	- - - -	Genesee.
James C. Smith,	- - - -	Canandaigua.
Amaziah B. James,	- - - -	Ogdensburg.
Erastus Corning,	- - - -	Albany.
Francis Granger,	- - - -	Canandaigua.
Greene C. Bronson,	- - - -	New York.
William E. Dodge,	- - - -	New York.
John A. King,	- - - -	Jamaica.
John E. Wool, -	- - - -	Troy.

NEW JERSEY.

Charles S. Olden,	- - - -	Princeton.
Peter D. Vroom,	- - - -	Trenton.
Robert F. Stockton,	- - - -	Princeton.
Benjamin Williamson, -	- - -	Elizabeth.
Joseph F. Randolph,	- - - -	Trenton.
Frederick T. Frelinghuysen,	- - -	Newark.
Rodman M. Price, -	- - - -	Harrison, Hudson Co.
William C. Alexander, -	- - - -	P. O. Broadway, N. Y.
Thomas J. Stryker,	- - - -	Trenton.

PENNSYLVANIA.

James Pollock, -	- - - -	Milton.
William M. Meredith,	- - - -	Philadelphia.
David Wilmot, -	- - - -	Towanda.
A. W. Loomis,	- - - -	Pittsburg.
Thomas E. Franklin,	- - - -	Lancaster.
William McKennan,	- - - -	Washington.
Thomas White, -	- - - -	Indiana.

DELAWARE.

George B. Rodney, -	- - - -	Newcastle.
Daniel M. Bates,	- - - -	Wilmington.
Henry Ridgely,	- - - -	Dover.
John W. Houston,	- - - -	Milford.
William Cannon,	- - - -	Bridgeville.

MARYLAND.

John F. Dent, - - - - -	Milestown.
Reverdy Johnson, - - - -	Baltimore.
John W. Crisfield, - - -	Princess Ann.
Augustus W. Bradford, - - -	Govanstown.
William T. Goldsborough, - - -	Cambridge.
J. Dixon Roman, - - - -	Hagerstown.
Benjamin C. Howard, - - -	Catonsville.

VIRGINIA.

John Tyler, - - - - -	Sherwood Forest.
William C. Rives, - - -	
John W. Brockenbrough, - -	Lexington.
George W. Summers, - - -	Kanawha C. H.
James A. Seddon, - - - -	

NORTH CAROLINA.

George Davis, - - - - -	Wilmington.
Thomas Ruffin, - - - -	Graham.
David S. Reid, - - - -	Pleasantville.
D. M. Barringer, - - -	Raleigh.
J. M. Morehead, - - -	Greensboro'.

TENNESSEE.

Samuel Milligan, - - -	Greenville.
Josiah M. Anderson, - - -	Walnut Valley.
Robert L. Caruthers, - -	Lebanon.
Thomas Martin, - - -	Pulaski.
Isaac R. Hawkins, - - -	Huntington.
A. W. O. Totten, - - -	Jackson.
R. J. McKinney, - - -	Knoxville.
Alvin Cullom, - - -	Livingston.
William P. Hickerson, - -	Manchester.
George W. Jones, - - -	Fayetteville.
F. K. Zollicoffer, - - -	Nashville.
William H. Stephens, - -	Jackson.

KENTUCKY.

William O. Butler, - - -	Carrollton.
James B. Clay, - - - -	Ashland.
Joshua F. Bell, - - -	Danville.
Charles S. Morehead, - -	Louisville.
James Guthrie, - - -	Louisville.
Charles A. Wickliffe, - -	Bardstown.

MISSOURI.

John D. Coalter, - - -	St. Louis.
Alexander W. Doniphan, - -	Liberty.
Waldo P. Johnson, - - -	Osceola.
Aylett H. Buckner, - -	Bowling-Green.
Harrison Hough, - - -	Charleston.

OHIO.

Salmon P. Chase, - - -	Columbus.
William S. Groesbeck, - - - -	Cincinnati.
Franklin T. Backus, - - - -	Cleveland.
Reuben Hitchcock, - - - - -	Cleveland.
Thomas Ewing, - - - - -	Lancaster.
V. B. Horton, - - - - -	Pomeroy.
C. P. Wolcott, - - - - -	Akron.

INDIANA.

Caleb B. Smith, - - - - -	Indianapolis.
Pleasant A. Hackleman, - - -	Rushville.
Godlove S. Orth, - - - -	Lafayette.
E. W. H. Ellis, - - - - -	Goshen.
Thomas C. Slaughter, - - - -	Corydon.

ILLINOIS.

John Wood, - - - - -	Quincy.
Stephen T. Logan, - - - -	Springfield.
John M. Palmer, - - - -	Carlinville.
Burton C. Cook, - - - - -	Ottowa.!
Thomas J. Turner, - - - -	Freeport.

IOWA.

James Harlan, - - - - -	Mt. Pleasant.
James W. Grimes, - - - - -	Burlington.
Samuel H. Curtis, - - - - -	Keokuk.
William Vandever, - - - -	Dubuque.

KANSAS.

Thomas Ewing, jr., - - - - -	Leavenworth.
J. C. Stone, - - - - -	Leavenworth.
H. J. Adams, - - - - -	Leavenworth.
M. F. Conway, - - - - -	Lawrence.

11

APPENDIX.

The delegates from the several States presented the following as the resolutions of their respective States, to be considered by the Convention; which were ordered to be printed, and made part of the journal :

TENNESSEE.

RESOLUTIONS proposing amendments to the Constitution of the United States.

Resolved by the General Assembly of the State of Tennessee, That a Convention of delegates from all the slaveholding States should assemble at Nashville, Tennessee, or such other place as a majority of the States co-operating may designate, on the 4th day of February, 1861, to digest and define a basis upon which, if possible, the Federal Union and the constitutional rights of the slave States may be perpetuated and preserved.

Resolved, That the General Assembly of the State of Tennessee appoint a number of delegates to said Convention, of our ablest and wisest men, equal to our whole delegation in Congress; and that the Governor of Tennessee immediately furnish copies of these resolutions to the Governors of the slaveholding States, and urge the participation of such States in said Convention.

Resolved, That in the opinion of this General Assembly, such plan of adjustment should embrace the following propositions as amendments to the Constitution of the United States :

1. A declaratory amendment that African slaves, as held under the institutions of the slaveholding States, shall be recognized as property, and entitled to the *status* of other property, in the States where slavery exists, in all places within the exclusive jurisdiction of Congress in the slave States, in all the Territories south of 36° 30', in the District of Columbia, in transit, and whilst temporarily sojourning with the owner in the non-slaveholding States and Territories north of 36° 30', and when fugitives from the owner, in the several places above named, as well as in all places in the exclusive jurisdiction of Congress in the non-slaveholding States.

2. That all the territory now owned, or which may be hereafter acquired, by the United States south of the parallel of 36° 30', African slavery shall be recognized as existing, and be protected by all the departments of the Federal and Territorial Governments, and in all north of that line, now owned, or to be acquired, it shall not be recognized as existing; and whenever States formed out of any of said territory south of said line, having a population equal to that of a congressional district, shall apply for admission into the Union, the same shall be admitted as slave States, whilst States north of the line, formed out of said territory, and having a population equal to a congressional district, shall be admitted without slavery; but the States formed out of said territory north and south having been admitted as members of the Union, shall have all the powers over the institution of slavery possessed by the other States of the Union.

3. Congress shall have no power to abolish slavery in places under its exclusive jurisdiction, and situate within the limits of States that permit the holding of slaves.

4. Congress shall have no power to abolish slavery within the District of Columbia, as long as it exists in the adjoining States of Virginia and Maryland, or either, nor without the consent of the inhabitants, nor without just compensation made to such owners of slaves as do not consent to such abolishment. Nor shall Congress at any time prohibit the officers of the Federal Government, or members of Congress whose duties require them to be in said District, from bringing with them their slaves, and holding them as such, during the time their duties may require them to remain there, and afterwards take them from the District.

5. Congress shall have no power to prohibit or hinder the transportation of slaves from one State to another, or the Territory in which slaves are by law permitted to be held, whether that transportation be by land, navigable rivers, or by seas.

6. In addition to the Fugitive Slave clause, provide that when a slave has been demanded of the Executive authority of the State to which he has fled, if he is not delivered, and the owner permitted to carry him out of the State in peace, the State so failing to deliver shall pay to the owner the value of such slave, and such damages as he may have sustained in attempting to reclaim his slave, and secure his right of action in the Supreme Court of the United States, with execution against the property of such State and the individuals thereof.

7. No future amendment of the Constitution shall affect the six preceding articles, nor the third paragraph of the second section of the first article of the Constitution, nor the third paragraph of the second section of the fourth article of the Constitution ; and no amendments shall be made to the Constitution which will authorize or give to Congress any power to abolish or interfere with slavery in any of the States by whose laws it is, or may be, allowed or permitted.

8. That slave property shall be rendered secure in transit through, or whilst temporarily sojourning in, non-slaveholding States or Territories, or in the District of Columbia.

9. An amendment to the effect that all fugitives are to be deemed those offending the laws within the jurisdiction of the State, and who escape therefrom to other States; and that it is the duty of each State to suppress armed invasions of another State.

Resolved, That said Convention of the slaveholding States having agreed upon a basis of adjustment satisfactory to themselves. should, in the opinion of this General Assembly, refer it to a Convention of all the States, slaveholding and non-slaveholding, in the manner following :

It should invite all States friendly to such plan of adjustment, to elect delegates in such manner as to reflect the popular will, to assemble in a Constitutional Convention of all the States North and South, to be held at Richmond, Virginia, on the —— day of February, 1861, to revise and perfect such plan of adjustment, for its reference for final ratification and adoption by a Convention of the States respectively.

Resolved, That should a plan of adjustment, satisfactory to the South, not be acceded to by a requisite number of States to perfect amendments to the Constitution of the United States, it is the opinion of this General Assembly that the slaveholding States should adopt for themselves the Constitution of the United States, with such amendments as may be satisfactory to the slaveholding States, and that they should invite into the Union with them all States of the North which are willing to abide such amended Constitution and frame of Government, severing at once all connections with States refusing such reasonable guarantees to our future safety; such renewed conditions of Federal Union being first submitted for ratification to Conventions of all the States respectively.

Resolved, That the Governor of the State of Tennessee furnish copies of these resolutions immediately to the Governors of the non-slaveholding States.

OHIO.

JOINT RESOLUTIONS of the General Assembly of the State of Ohio, relative to the appointment of Commissioners to the Convention to meet in Washington on the 4th of February, proximo. Passed January 30, 1861.

WHEREAS, The Commonwealth of Virginia has appointed five Commissioners to meet in the city of Washington on the 4th day of February next, with similar Commissioners from other States, and after full and free conference to agree. if practicable, upon some adjustment of the unhappy difficulties now dividing our country, which may be alike satisfactory and honorable to the States concerned ; therefore, be it

Resolved by the General Assembly of the State of Ohio, That the Governor, by and with the advice and consent of the Senate, be, and he is hereby, authorized and empowered to appoint five Commissioners to represent the State of Ohio in said Conference.

Resolved, That while we are not prepared to assent to the terms of settlement proposed by Virginia, and are fully satisfied that the Constitution of the United States as it is, if fairly interpreted and obeyed by all sections of our country, contains ample provisions within itself for the correction of all evils complained of, yet a disposition to reciprocate the patriotic spirit of a sister State, and a sincere desire to have harmoniously adjusted all differences between us, induce us to favor the appointment of the Commission as requested.

Resolved, That the Governor be requested to transmit without delay a copy of these resolutions to each of the Commissioners to be appointed as aforesaid, to the end that they may repair to the City of Washington, on the day hereinbefore named, to meet such Commissioners as may be appointed by any of the States in accordance with the aforesaid propositions of Virginia.

Resolved, That in the opinion of this General Assembly, it will be wise and expedient to adjourn the proposed Convention to a later day, and that the Commissioners to be appointed as aforesaid, are requested to use their influence in procuring an adjournment to the 4th day of April next.

KENTUCKY.

RESOLUTIONS appointing Commissioners to attend a Conference at Washington City, February 4th, in accordance with the invitation of the Virginia Legislature.

WHEREAS, The General Assembly of Virginia, with a view to make an effort to preserve the Union and the Constitution in the spirit in which they were established by the fathers of the Republic, have, by resolution, invited all the States who are willing to unite with her in an earnest effort to adjust the present unhappy controversies, to appoint Commissioners to meet on the 4th of February next, to consider, and if practicable, agree upon some suitable adjustment—

Resolved, That we heartily accept the invitation of our Old Mother Virginia, and that the following six Commissioners, viz: Wm. O. Butler, Jas. B. Clay, Joshua F. Bell, C. S. Morehead, Jas. Guthrie, and Chas. A. Wickliffe, be appointed to represent the State of Kentucky in the contemplated Convention, whose duty it shall be to repair to the city of Washington, on the day designated, to meet such Commissioners as may be appointed by any of the States in accordance with the foregoing invitation.

Resolved, That if said Commissioners shall agree upon any plan of adjustment requiring amendments to the Federal Constitution, they be requested to communicate the proposed amendments to Congress, for the purpose of having the same submitted by that body, according to the forms of the Constitution, to the several States for ratification.

Resolved, That if said Commissioners cannot agree in an adjustment, or if agreeing, Congress shall refuse to submit for ratification such amendments as they may propose, the Commissioners of this State shall immediately communicate the result to the Executive of this Commonwealth, to be by him laid before this General Assembly.

Resolved, That in the opinion of the General Assembly of Kentucky, the propositions embraced in the resolutions presented to the Senate of the United States by the Hon. John J. Crittenden, so construed that the first article proposed as an amendment to the Constitution of the United States shall apply to all the territory of the United States now held or hereafter acquired south of latitude 36 deg. and 30 min., and provide that slavery of the African race shall be effectually protected as property herein during the continuance of the Territorial Government; and the fourth article shall secure to the owners of slaves the right of transit with their slaves between and through the non-slaveholding States and Territories, constitute the basis of such an adjustment of the unhappy controversy which now divides the States of this Confederacy, as would be acceptable to the people of this Commonwealth.

Resolved, That the Governor be, and he is hereby, requested to communicate information of the foregoing appointment to the Commissioners above named, at as early a day as practicable, and that he also communicate copies of the foregoing resolutions to the Executives of the respective States.

INDIANA.

A JOINT RESOLUTION authorizing the Governor to appoint Commissioners to meet those sent by other States in Convention on the state of the Union.

WHEREAS, The State of Virginia has transmitted to this State resolutions adopted by her General Assembly, inviting all such States as are willing to unite with her in an earnest effort to adjust the unhappy controversies, in the spirit in which the Constitution was originally formed, to send Commissioners to meet those appointed by that State in Convention, to be held in the city of Washington, on the fourth day of February next, to consider, and if possible, to agree upon some suitable adjustment :

And whereas, some of the States to which invitations were extended by the State of Virginia have already responded and appointed their Commissioners: therefore,

Resolved by the General Assembly of the State of Indiana, That we accept the invitation of the State of Virginia, in the true spirit of fraternal feeling, and that the Governor of the State is hereby directed and empowered to appoint five Commissioners to meet the Commissioners appointed by our sister States, to consult upon the unhappy differences now dividing the country; but the said Commissioners shall take no action that will commit this State until *nineteen* of the States are represented, nor without first having communicated with this General Assembly in regard to such action, and having received the authority of the same so to commit the State.

Resolved, That while we are not prepared to assent to the terms of settlement proposed by the State of Virginia, and are fully satisfied that the Constitution, if fairly interpreted and obeyed, contains ample provision within itself for the correction of the evils complained of; still, with a disposition to reciprocate the patriotic desire of the State of Virginia, and to have harmoniously adjusted all differences existing between the States of the Union, this General Assembly is induced to respond to the invitation of Virginia, by the appointment of the Commissioners herein provided for; but as the time fixed for the Convention to assemble is so near at hand that the States cannot all be represented, it is expected that the Commissioners on behalf of this State will insist that the Convention adjourn until such time as the States shall have an opportunity of being represented.

Resolved, That his Excellency, the Governor, be requested to transmit copies of these resolutions to the Executives of each of the States of the Union.

DELAWARE.

JOINT RESOLUTIONS appointing Commissioners.

WHEREAS, The State of Virginia has recommended the holding of a Convention of Delegates from all the States of the Union, at the City of Washington, on the 4th day of February next, for the purpose of taking into consideration and perfecting some plan of adjusting the matters of controversy now so unhappily subsisting in the family of States, and has appointed five Commissioners to represent the people of that Commonwealth in said Convention ; and

Whereas, the people of the State of Delaware regard the preservation of the Union as paramount to any political consideration, and are fixed in their determination that Delaware, the first to adopt the Federal Constitution, will be the last to do any act tending to destroy the integrity of the Union; therefore,

Be it resolved by the Senate and House of Representatives of the State of Delaware in General Assembly met, That the Hon. George B. Rodney, Daniel M. Bates, Esq., Dr. Henry Ridgley, Hon. John W. Houston, and William Cannon, Esq., be, and they are hereby, appointed Commissioners, on behalf of the State of Delaware, to represent the people of said State in the Convention to be held at Washington, on the fourth day of February next.

Resolved, That in the opinion of this General Assembly, the people of Delaware are thoroughly devoted to the perpetuity of the Union, and that the Commissioners appointed by the foregoing resolution are expected to emulate the example set by the immortal patriots who framed the Federal Constitution, by sacrificing all minor considerations upon the altar of the Union.

Resolved further, That it shall be the duty of the Secretary of State to furnish a copy of the above preamble and resolutions to each of the Commissioners herein and hereby appointed, duly attested under the great seal of the State.

Resolved further, That immediately upon the adoption of the foregoing preamble and resolutions, it shall be the duty of the Clerk of the House to transmit to the Secretary of State a copy thereof, certified by him; and when the Secretary of State shall have received said copy so certified, it shall be evidence that said preamble and resolutions were duly adopted by this General Assembly.

ILLINOIS.

Whereas, Resolutions of the State of Virginia have been communicated to the General Assembly of this State, proposing the appointment of Commissioners by the several States to meet in convention, on the 4th day of February, A. D. 1861, at Washington.

Resolved by the Senate, the House of Representatives concurring herein, That with the earnest desire for the return of harmony and kind relations among all our sister States, and out of respect to the Commonwealth of Virginia, the Governor of this State be requested to appoint five Commissioners on the part of the State of Illinois, to confer and consult with the Commissioners of other States who shall meet at Washington: *Provided,* That said Commissioners shall at all times be subject to the control of the General Assembly of the State of Illinois.

Resolved, That the appointment of Commissioners by the State of Illinois, in response to the invitation of the State of Virginia, is *not* an expression of opinion on the part of this State that any amendment of the Federal Constitution is requisite to secure to the people of the slaveholding States adequate guarantees for the security of their rights, nor an approval of the basis of settlement of our difficulties proposed by the State of Virginia, but it is an expression of our willingness to unite with the State of Virginia in an earnest effort to adjust the present unhappy controversies in the spirit in which the Constitution was originally formed, and consistently with its principles.

Resolved, That while we are willing to appoint Commissioners to meet in convention with those of other States for consultation upon matters which at present distract our harmony as a nation, we also insist that the appropriate and constitutional method of considering and acting upon the grievances complained of by our sister States, would be by the call of a convention for the amendment of the Constitution in the manner contemplated by the fifth article of that instrument; and if the States deeming themselves aggrieved, shall request Congress to call such convention, the Legislature of Illinois will and does concur in such call.

NEW JERSEY.

JOINT RESOLUTIONS in relation to the Union of the States.

Whereas, The people of New Jersey, conforming to the opinion of "the Father of his Country," consider the unity of the government, which constitutes the people of the United States one people, a main pillar in the edifice of their independence, the support of their tranquility at home and peace abroad, of their prosperity, and of that liberty which they so highly prize; and properly estimating the immense value of their National Union to their individual happiness, they cherish a cordial, habitual, and immovable attachment to it as the palladium of their political safety and prosperity; therefore,

1. *Be it resolved by the Senate and General Assembly of the State of New Jersey,* That it is the duty of every good citizen, in all suitable and proper ways, to stand by and sustain the Union of the States as transmitted to us by our fathers.

2. *And be it resolved,* That the government of the United States is a national government, and the Union it was designed to perfect is not a mere compact or league; and that the Constitution was adopted in a spirit of mutual compromise and concession by the people of the United States, and can only be preserved by the constant recognition of that spirit.

3. *And be it resolved*, That however undoubted may be the right of the general government to maintain its authority and enforce its laws over all parts of the country, it is equally certain that forbearance and compromise are indispensable at this crisis to the perpetuity of the Union, and that it is the dictate of reason, wisdom, and patriotism peacefully to adjust whatever differences exist between the different sections of the country.

4. *And be it resolved*, That the resolutions and propositions submitted to the Senate of the United States by the Hon. John J. Crittenden, of Kentucky, for the compromise of the questions in dispute between the people of the Northern and of the Southern States, or any other constitutional method that will permanently settle the question of slavery, will be acceptable to the people of the State of New Jersey, and the Senators and Representatives in Congress from New Jersey be requested and earnestly urged to support those resolutions and propositions.

5. *And be it resolved*, That as the Union of the States is in imminent danger unless the remedies before suggested be speedily adopted, then, as a last resort, the State of New Jersey hereby makes application, according to the terms of the Constitution, of the Congress of the United States, to call a convention (of the States) to propose amendments to said Constitution.

6. *And be it resolved*, That such of the States as have in force laws which interfere with the constitutional rights of citizens of the other States, either in regard to their persons or property, or which militate against the just construction of that part of the Constitution that provides that " the citizens of each State shall be entitled to all the privileges and immunities of citizens in the several States," are earnestly urged and requested, for the sake of peace and the Union, to repeal all such laws.

7. *And be it resolved*, That His Excellency, Charles S. Olden, Peter D. Vroom, Robert F. Stockton, Benjamin Williamson, Joseph F. Randolph, Frederick T. Frelinghuysen, Rodman M. Price, William C. Alexander, and Thomas J. Stryker, be appointed commissioners to confer with Congress and our sister States, and urge upon them the importance of carrying into effect the principles and objects of the foregoing resolutions.

8. *And be it resolved*, That the commissioners above named, in addition to their other powers, be authorized to meet with those now or hereafter to be appointed by our sister State of Virginia, and such commissioners of other States as have been, or may be hereafter appointed, to meet at Washington on the fourth day of February next.

9. *And be it resolved*, That copies of the foregoing resolutions be sent to the President of the Senate and Speaker of the House of Representatives of the United States, and to the Senators and Representatives in Congress from New Jersey, and to the Governors of the several States.

NEW YORK.

CONCURRENT RESOLUTIONS appointing commissioners from this State to meet commissioners from other States at Washington, on invitation of Virginia.

WHEREAS, The State of Virginia, by resolutions of her General Assembly, passed the 19th instant, has invited such of the slaveholding and non-slaveholding States as are willing to unite with her to meet at Washington on the 4th of February next, to consider, and, if practicable, agree on some suitable adjustment of our national difficulties ; and whereas, the people of New York, while they hold the opinion that the Constitution of the United States, as it is, contains all needful guarantees for the rights of the States, are, nevertheless, ready at all times to confer with their brethren upon all alleged grievances, and to do all that can justly be required of them to allay discontent : therefore,

Resolved, That David Dudley Field, Wm. Curtis Noyes, James S. Wadsworth, Jas. C. Smith, Amaziah B. James, Erastus Corning, Addison Gardiner, Greene C. Bronson, Wm. E. Dodge, ex-Governor John A. King, and Major General John E. Wool, be, and are hereby, appointed commissioners, on the part of this State, to meet Commissioners from other States in the city of Washington on the 4th day of February next, or so soon thereafter as Commissioners shall be appointed by a majority of the States of the Union, to confer with them upon the complaints of any part of the country, and to suggest such remedies therefor as to them shall seem fit and proper ; but the said Commissioners shall, at all times, be subject to the control of this Legislature, and shall cast five votes, to be determined by a majority of their number.

Resolved, That in thus acceding to the request of Virginia, it is not to be understood that this Legislature approve of the propositions submitted by the General Assembly of that State, or concedes the propriety of their adoption by the proposed Convention. But while adhering to the position she has heretofore occupied, New York will not reject an invitation to a conference, which, by bringing together the men of both sections, holds out the possibility of an honorable settlement of our national difficulties, and the restoration of peace and harmony to the country.

Resolved, That the Governor be requested to transmit a copy of the foregoing resolutions to the Executives of the several States, and also to the President of the United States, and to inform the Commissioners without delay of their appointment.

Resolved, That the foregoing resolutions be transmitted to the honorable the Senate, with a request that they concur therein.

PENNSYLVANIA.

RESOLUTIONS to appoint Commissioners to a Convention of the States.

Whereas, the Legislature of the State of Virginia has invited a meeting of Commissioners from the several States of this Union, to be held in the city of Washington, on the 4th day of February next, to consider, and if practicable, agree upon some suitable adjustment of the unhappy differences which now disturb the business of the country and threaten the dissolution of this Union :

And whereas, in the opinion of this Legislature, no reasonable cause exists for this extraordinary excitement which now pervades some of the States, in relation to their domestic institutions, and while Pennsylvania still adheres to, and cannot surrender the principles which she has always entertained on the subject of slavery, this Legislature is willing to accept the invitation of Virginia, and unite with her in an earnest effort to restore the peace of the country, by such means as may be consistent with the principles upon which the Constitution is founded ; therefore,

Resolved by the Senate and House of Representatives of the Commonwealth of Pennsylvania in General Assembly met, That the invitation of the Legislature of Virginia to her sister States, for the appointment of Commissioners to meet in the city of Washington, on the fourth of February next, be, and the same is hereby, accepted ; and that the Governor be, and he is hereby, authorized to appoint seven Commissioners for the State of Pennsylvania, whose duty it shall be to repair to the city of Washington, on the day designated, to meet such Commissioners as may be appointed by any other States, which have not authorized or sanctioned the seizure of the forts, arsenals, or other property of the United States, to consider, and if possible, to agree upon suitable measures for the prompt and final settlement of the difficulties which now exist : *Provided,* That the said Commissioners shall be subject, in all their proceedings, to the instructions of this Legislature.

Resolved, That in the opinion of this Legislature, the people of Pennsylvania do not desire any alteration or amendment of the Constitution of the United States, and any recommendation from this body to that effect, while it does not come within its appropriate and legitimate duties, would not meet with their approval ; that Pennsylvania will cordially unite with the other States of the Union in the adoption of any proper constitutional measures adequate to guarantee and secure a more strict and faithful observance of the second section of the fourth article of the Constitution of the United States, which provides, among other things, that "the citizens of each State shall be entitled to all privileges and immunities of citizens of the several States," and that no person held to service or labor in one State under the law thereof, escaping into another, shall in consequence of any law or regulation therein, be discharged from such service or labor, but shall be delivered up on the claim of the party to whom such service or labor may be due.

MASSACHUSETTS.

RESOLVE for the appointment of Commissioners to attend a Convention to be held in the city of Washington.

Whereas, The Commonwealth of Massachusetts is desirous of a full and free conference with the General Government, and with any or all of the other States of the Union, at any time, and on every occasion, when such conference may promote the welfare of the country ; and whereas, questions of grave moment have arisen touching the powers of the Government and the relations between the different States of the Union ; and whereas, the State of Virginia has expressed a desire to meet her sister States in Convention at Washington : therefore,

Resolved, That the Governor of this Commonwealth, by and with the advice and consent of the council, be, and he hereby is authorized, to appoint seven persons as Commissioners, to proceed to Washington to confer with the General Government, or with the separate States, or with any association of delegates from such States, and to report their doings to the Legislature at its present session ; it being expressly declared that their acts shall be at all times under the control, and subject to the approval or rejection, of the Legislature.

RHODE ISLAND.

Whereas, The General Assembly of the Commonwealth of Virginia, on the 19th day of January inst., adopted resolutions inviting the sister States of this Union to appoint Commissioners to meet on the 4th day of February next in the city of Washington, to consider the practicability of agreeing on terms of adjustment of our present national troubles :

Resolved, That the Governor be, and he is hereby authorized, to appoint five Commissioners, on the part of this State, to meet such Commissioners as may be appointed by other States, in the city of Washington on the 4th day of February next, to consider, and, if practicable, agree upon some amicable adjustment of the present unhappy national difficulties, upon the basis and in the spirit of the Constitution of the United States.

MISSOURI.

JOINT RESOLUTION to appoint Commissioners.

Resolved by the House of Representatives, the Senate concurring therein, That Waldo P. Johnson, John D. Coalter, A. W. Doniphan, Harrison Hough, and A. H. Buckner, be appointed Commissioners, on the part of the State of Missouri, to meet Commissioners from Virginia, and other States, in Convention at Washington city on the 4th of February, 1861, to endeavor to agree upon some plan of adjustment of existing difficulties, so as to preserve or to reconstruct the Union of these States, and to secure the honor and equal rights of the slaveholding States. Said Commissioners shall always be under the control of the General Assembly, except when the State Convention shall be in session, during which time they shall be under the control of the Convention.

REPORT

OF THE

KENTUCKY COMMISSIONERS

TO THE LATE

PEACE CONFERENCE HELD AT WASHINGTON CITY,

MADE TO THE LEGISLATURE OF KENTUCKY.

FRANKFORT, KY.:
PRINTED AT THE YEOMAN OFFICE.
JNO. B. MAJOR, STATE PRINTER.
1861.

www.ingramcontent.com/pod-product-compliance
Lightning Source LLC
Chambersburg PA
CBHW022013050726
47499CB00007BA/2558